The story that I intended to eat them is a fabrication. People will make up anything. I did intend to observe them closely under conditions of stress, and more blood would have been very useful to me.

In the end, I would probably have let them go back home. Their father, my husband, was making my life as wretched as his own. In the end, it would have been a choice between having the children back and pretending (for a while) to be a happy-ever-after fairy-tale family, or getting rid of all three of them and moving on.

ROX

TRULY GRIM TALES

PRISCILLA GALLOWAY

LAUREL-LEAF BOOKS

Published by
Bantam Doubleday Dell Books for Young Readers
a division of
Bantam Doubleday Dell Publishing Group, Inc.
1540 Broadway
New York, New York 10036

Visit us on the Web! www.bdd.com

**Educators and librarians, visit the BDD Teacher's
Resource Center at www.bdd.com/teachers**

ISBN: 0-440-22728-3

RL: 5.9

Reprinted by arrangement with Delacorte Press

Printed in the United States of America

November 1998

10 9 8 7 6 5 4 3 2 1

OPM

To my beloved husband,
Howard Collum

CONTENTS

ACKNOWLEDGMENTS

Whoever plays with the grand old stories owes a huge debt to centuries of storytellers who have gone before, those who have told and retold, and those who have written down and collected. They have given me such delight, and so much to ponder. Nonetheless, I've always known they left out a lot and were unaware of even more. It has not been easy to discover the truth, but I have persisted. Gradually the stories behind the stories have come clear.

On a more mundane level, I thank all the people who have loved my *Truly Grim Tales* over the years of their creation and have kept encouraging me to persist toward publication, and I bless the enthusiasm of David and Lynn Bennett, of the Transatlantic Literary Agency, Inc., who brought the tales to the right publishers and to the right editor: Mary Cash, editorial director of Bantam Doubleday Dell Books for Young Readers.

THE NAME

My mother I never knew. She was sickly after my birth and died when I was two years old. My week-old sister died too. Now I am certain that my father should have married again. At the time, like every child, I wanted only to have all his attention, all his time, all his love. Roomfuls of expensive toys, bevies of hired nursemaids served only to convince me (especially during my father's frequent absences) that I was the loneliest child in the world.

Early memory brings dinner served at night in the great hall. The carved table seated forty guests, but only two of us dined there: Father at one end, his slender face partly hidden by the silver candelabra, and I at the other. My chair was of dark wood, built high especially for me. I used to curl my fingers into its deep carving. Tall footmen in livery served endless dishes. I sat and listened to my father. "You bear a proud name," he told me again and again, "the oldest name in the land. See that you are a credit to it."

"Yes, sir," I would say, as loudly as I could, with my shoulders back like a man, or as much like a man as I could manage.

Only his sister ever argued with him. "Pel should be having nursery tea for the next ten years," she said. "A child needs a real childhood."

"If you don't like my ways, don't darken my door, Amelia," my father told her.

"Please, Father, I like having dinner with you," I said. Father smiled grimly, and Aunt Amelia ordered her carriage and left.

After dinner, Father and I would sit by the fire in the library. I had the run of the place and could take down any book from the shelves. Father merely smiled his thin smile if I dropped one of the great leather tomes that were almost as heavy as I was myself. I could see that he was pleased I did not ask for help, either from him or from one of the servants. I do not remember a time when I could not read, though I had no teacher. "Read widely and observe closely," Father said. "Later, perhaps, you shall go away to school."

I never wanted to go away. I was small, smaller than the village children, and never grew very much. None of that mattered until shortly after my tenth birthday. Disease swept through the countryside that summer, killing many children and leaving others with a dragging leg or a useless arm. It did not spare our great home. I shall never forget the pain. Worse than the pain was the terror that I would not be able to breathe, that I would die of suffocation. I clung to the doctor, to the housekeeper, to any human presence in my room, and could not be pried loose.

My father came only once. He himself tore my desperate hands from his arm. In his eyes I saw both fear and shame. "Be a man" was all he said.

Later, when I was well enough to be carried to the library, he watched from the gallery. He dictated that I should eat henceforth in my own rooms. A crippled son! How could I carry on The Name?

Slowly I regained the use of one leg. Slowly I gained strength in the other. Although I finally threw away my crutches, my limp and the tilt of my body became worse with the years. My right leg continued to grow. My left leg did not. I was thankful when all growth ceased, however short I might be.

Perhaps my father refused to see me because he loved me and was pained by the sight of my crippled body. Sometimes today I manage to consider this possibility. Mostly I felt the desolation of being abandoned, alone and unloved at ten years of age. He was a proud man, my father. He could bear almost anything except pity. Other people might have pitied him on my account, but he gave them no opportunity. Unsocial he had always been; now he became a recluse.

I was desolate. Ill, crippled, and deprived of all companionship, I kept to my rooms at first. After some months, I took my crutches and ventured out into the estate. I carried crumbs of bread and befriended the ducks on the pond. In time I learned to be so silent and still that a fawn would dare to approach.

Later still, after the need for crutches had disappeared, I would wander with my book to the riverbank above the millrace, letting sun and water heal my spirit and bring strength to my body. There one day a nymph appeared, a maiden all golden curls and dimples.

Can anyone in these wicked times believe in love, innocent love, adoring love, love without hesitation? It happened to us both, that is the miracle. Thinking later, I knew I looked like a lord, even in my old shirt and breeks, there in the sweet grass, with my back against a sturdy oak. "Oh," she murmured, "how beautiful," and bent to my lips. I caught her hands, and there was no turning back. She never winced or turned away even for a moment when she later saw my hobbled walk, my mismatched legs.

"She's simple," the villagers said, feeling sorry for the miller's son, to whom she had been promised in marriage as a child. Their mothers had been childhood friends, but the girl had not grown up in the village and the miller's son was taking his time about the wedding, not sure that he would go through with it.

It was not easy for me to get the information about her that I craved, but I had learned to dissemble well. Certainly none of the servants knew my interest in the gossip they told.

How could I marry her myself? I wondered. How could I gain my father's consent? It would not be easy. Before my illness, he had half-arranged a match with an earl's daughter. If I raised the question of marriage, he would no doubt insist on the marriage he had planned. The earl might object to a crippled son-in-law, but likely not, my looks being less important than my estates and my ability to father an heir.

Meanwhile, I wanted only my golden girl, and loved her by the riverbank in the sweet grass. Summer was forever. Wild plans for the future half-formed in my head, but never seemed real or possible. My darling lived only in the present, and happily, lovingly so. I joined her there.

It came to an end when her pregnancy began to show. Then I had to force an interview with my father. "Rejoice, Father," I told him, "a child grows, begotten of my body."

He made inquiries. "I will not see her," he wrote to me, "nor you again unless I must. The girl is a simpleton who can barely say her name, they tell me, and writes and reads not at all. Who knows if you are the father of her expected child? The miller's son must wed her. I will provide her dowry. Thus it shall be."

And thus it was. Try as I would, I could not stand against my father's will and power. The village was drunk for three days at my father's expense, and a new mill and granary were built, as well as a cottage for the happy couple. When the child was born a few months later, it was a week before I knew. I did not seek out my darling. Surely she had forgotten me already, living in the present of her new baby and her new life. I would not trouble her tender heart.

But my own pain was greater than in my illness. I could not stay in my luxurious rooms. My feet took

me into the hills, into the forest. Wandering aim-
lessly, I came upon a simple stone hut. The roof had
fallen in long since, but the walls were sound. I had
not been trained to manual work, but set myself to
construct a roof that would withstand the elements,
and succeeded tolerably well. Some winter snow
blew in, and my hut was always either smoky or cold
(sometimes both), but it suited me. There I stayed.
A shepherd boy was persuaded, for a small fee, to
bring me simple food. To fill the long hours I
chopped wood, and was surprised to find that when
my funds ran low I could support myself with this
labor. I did not need my father after all. Perhaps I
could have run off with my golden girl. Perhaps we
could have had our child.

Thinking thus, I would batter the great logs with
my ax until exhaustion put an end to thought and
feeling both.

Seasons passed, and years.

One winter day my shepherd, now a grown man,
lingered in the shelter of my hut. He had brought
my supplies as usual, neither of us expecting the
sudden storm. "The old lord is dying," he told me.
"Criers are out everywhere to seek his son and
heir."

I waited for some feeling in me to emerge: bitter-
ness perhaps, sorrow, even joy, but nothing stirred
except a faint curiosity. It was enough. I could go
and see him and be untouched.

Curiosity was still dominant when I approached
his bed the following day. It had not been difficult to
convince the household of my identity, though

twenty years had passed. My legs had grown stronger but had not changed their disproportion. My body, though lithe and muscled, was more twisted. The soft shirt felt strange against my callused palms. "Forgive me, my son," whispered the shrunken figure on the bed. "Forgive."

How he hated pity, my father, but no other feeling was possible. "I forgive you," I told him, and again, "I forgive."

Forgiveness came easily to my lips then, but it was fortunate that my father died that night, before I began to discover what had happened, before my rage began to rise. Years before, I discovered, the old miller had died and the son had taken his place. He came now to the great hall where my father's body lay in state, paying his respects along with everybody else, great and small. He had grown fat and gray. His belly walked before him. I did not know him. I scanned every female face, waiting to see my beloved. I could not have failed to recognize her, no matter how much she had changed. She did not appear.

I could not chance damaging her reputation by direct inquiries. It was several days before I pieced together the story, the repeated beatings, the ugly death. Accidental, the judge had ruled, but my darling was surefooted by day or night. I knew she would never have fallen to her death down a flight of stairs. The miller was warned to take good care of his baby daughter. No further accidents would be tolerated.

"His" daughter! I sent for both of them immediately, but they were gone. They had left that very afternoon for the city. "The miller is taking a special fine white flour to the king himself," my courier said in awe. "His daughter is to be presented, along with other young ladies. She is very beautiful, even though her father is only a miller."

I had never been presented myself and had no friends at court. I rode badly and painfully. I possessed no clothes suitable for society. Nonetheless, I took horse immediately, accompanied by two servants. The carriage would have been easier, but I could not wait. This time, things would go *my* way.

My haste was warranted. Was that miller vengeful or just greedy? The fool! He had told the king that she could spin straw into gold. The king—another fool—had locked her and her spinning wheel into a room full of straw, vowing to have her executed next morning if the straw had not been turned into gold. His chamberlain was having a scaffold erected. "Nobody can spin straw into gold," the watchers said. "We might as well be here early for the hanging."

Then I blessed the old servant who had urged me to take gold and had shown me my father's treasure chest. It was not easy to bribe my way in to see the maiden, but gold can work miracles at need. She sat there in tears, head bent over her wheel. "Look at me," I ordered. Slowly her face was raised to mine. It could have been her mother's face, young again, a little narrower, but her eyes were gray like mine instead of her mother's blue. Holding back my own tears was the hardest thing I have ever done.

"I can help you," I said at last, my voice rough with the unshed tears. "Give me your necklace."

I held it in my hands, a pretty bauble of green glass beads, warmed by her white neck.

It was well for me that the guards knew their king for a fool. They delighted in removing the straw and carrying in the heavy bags of gold coin. "It doesn't look much like it's been spun," one of them told me, "but he's so greedy he won't care."

And so it was. The king was delighted. "You are the most wonderful spinner in the world," he told her. "Do it again tonight. We'll leave the scaffold up just in case, but I'm sure you won't fail."

I had suspected that something of the sort might happen and had sent my men home for more gold. Just as well. This was a larger room, with more straw. The guards were happy to go along with me again. "She's a pretty thing," one of them said to me. "She wouldn't look nearly so good with a stretched neck."

"No," I agreed through clenched teeth.

Again she was weeping, but her head came up quickly as I touched her shoulder. I could see the hope in her eyes. "Give me your ring," I told her. It was a pearl, set in a narrow band of gold.

"It was my mother's," she told me.

"It was," I agreed, but did not tell her that I had given her mother the pretty thing.

Again we exchanged straw for coin, and again the king laughed and praised her for spinning straw into gold. "Do it one more time and I'll marry you," he told her, leading her past the scaffold to a third straw-filled room, bigger than the other two put together.

It would take all my remaining gold to make a decent show in that room, but I did not hesitate. "What must I give you this time?" the maiden asked. "I have nothing else."

Nor have I, if the king does this trick one more time, I thought but did not say. "Give me your first-born child," I told her.

She looked away from me, shuddering a little. Her eyes fixed on the window. My eyes followed hers. Outside, the gallows made a black "L" upside down against the rising moon.

"If I live, and if I have a child," she replied.

It did not seem a great thing at the time.

Again the king was pleased. Happily, he demanded no more spun-gold bars, but married the miller's daughter, my daughter, as he had vowed to do.

I sold an heirloom or two and made my bow at court in time to be invited to the wedding. A costly gift was expected—nay, required. Mine was a carousel, a music box of gold and ivory, inlaid with lapis and pearl. When it was wound, the ivory and ebony horses pranced, riding up and down their golden poles, and a tiny diamond-and-sapphire-studded ballerina danced bareback on the leading horse. The carousel had been my grandmother's christening gift, and I loved it above all my family possessions. It seemed right that it should go now to my daughter, even though she did not know me for her sire.

At the wedding, I was on tenterhooks to see

whether she would recognize me as the one who had saved her life. My lame leg and off-balance body are distinctive, as is my diminutive stature. But I need not have feared. In the straw-filled rooms, I had been dressed in sober black, and she had looked up at me through her tears. Those rooms were somber, each one lit dimly by one small window through which the scaffold loomed, menacing us both.

Now darkness had turned to light. The great hall of the palace was bathed in sun from high clerestory windows. Like all the guests, I glittered in jeweled robes. From her dais the young queen smiled graciously at everyone in turn, including me when at last I bent my head before her. She did not know me, although she thanked me a thousand times for my gift, which she said she loved and valued above all others, "except my husband's, of course," she added carefully. I was relieved and disappointed at the same time, but it was safer this way for us both.

Afterward my ancestral home was so lonely I could not bear it, and after a month of trying to wear elegant clothes and eat extravagant dinners, after a month of trying to read in a library where I seemed always to hear an echo of my father's pronouncements, I went back to my hut in the woods and to my simple life. Winter's cold winds were mine by right.

No one came to my hut, no one knew of its existence except my shepherd supplier, who over the years had also become my friend, if one can call it that. We talked little, but our silences were companionable. I liked him to share my fire. In the spring, in lambing time, he told me that the queen too had borne a child. Bonfires were lit in rejoicing throughout the land. I smiled, thinking of that baby, my own grandchild.

It was time to return to my great hall. Preparations were necessary. A wet nurse had to be hired and a nursery outfitted. I had not seriously thought it would ever happen, and it had happened. This time I went to court by carriage, carrying a bassinet lined with silk and embroidered with rosebuds and golden leaves. This time there was no hurry.

In the fullness of summer, I came to the young queen.

This time I wore the same black cloak I had worn in the spinning rooms, the same three-cornered hat. Her face turned ashen. She put her hands behind her, interposing her slight body between the cradle and me.

I held out my arms. She shook her head, kept shaking it, gasping like a fish landed on the riverbank, knowing it will never again dart carefree in the cool comfort of the stream. "My mother died young," she gasped at last, breathless. "I never had a creature, any creature, to love."

It was no easier for me to speak than for her. "Your promise," I croaked at last. "Give me the child."

Suddenly she was on her knees, clutching my hands. "Anything else, anything, my life if need be." I felt the ordeal, the sharpened spear in each word, and pushed her aside with leaden arms. Trembling, I lifted the sleeping child and looked in wonder at the long, dark eyelashes, at the miraculous whorls of a tiny, exquisite ear. The mother was beside me at once, but no more desirous than I of interrupting that sweet sleep. We looked down together on the tender face.

"You love her too," the mother softly exclaimed.

"I love her too," I agreed.

"Then it's easy. You love her. You could not, would not, tear her from her mother's arms."

"I was torn from mine," said I, "and you from yours."

Her eyes blazed into mine. "You cannot do it."

My daughter! How I loved her, the tiger fighting for her cub. In that moment, I was ready to lose my grandchild, as I had lost my mother and my mate. The moment passed. "Tell me my name," I told her lightly. "If in three days you can tell me my name, you shall keep your child." Handing her the infant, I turned abruptly on my heel.

Why did I do that? I asked myself on the drive to my rented lodgings. Why on earth did I do that?

To buy time, I answered myself. Time. To decide.

Three people: her, me, the child. Four: include the child's father the king, a foolish, greedy man. Five: include the miller, the child's acknowledged grandfather, a wife-beater, perhaps a child-beater too, given any opportunity.

Could I be happy, raising the child in the shadow of her despair? Could I find any value in living if I had no child to cherish? What would be better for the child? To be raised by a loving mother and a dangerous, foolish, greedy, unpredictable, sometimes cruel father? To be raised in the shadow of the throne? To be raised by an old man? (A wise old man, a loving old man, but an old man nonetheless.) I warmed my daughter's necklace in my hands.

I went back to her the following day with no clear answer in my own heart. For three hours, she named names: Michael, Samuel, Aaron, Peter, Bill, Will, William. Do short forms count?

My name is of elvish origin. She never came even remotely close. I felt the force of her will, but again could make no decision.

Again the next day I presented myself. This time she had sent messengers far and wide, she told me. Surely no name could have been missed! Her gray eyes were moist with hope and fear. "Highbothom, Dauoodaset, Running Elk, Shortribs, Caliban," she began. This time she took five hours of guesses. I substituted headshakes for words when my throat began to choke on "No."

I had sent for my shepherd friend the day before. He greeted me when I again reached my lodgings. He would be the ideal person to send to her with my name, should I choose to give it to her. The sins of the fathers shall be visited upon the sons, even unto the seventh generation. I had learned bitterly that those words were not the ravings of a vengeful God but were rather a statement of fact: how long it takes for evil to become neutralized, to be turned perhaps to good.

She will be an amazing child, that baby. Even as I

held her tiny body (could it have been only yesterday?), I could feel the strength of her will, feel it even through her sleep.

Tonight my decision must be made. What is best? What is best?

Tonight I must decide to leave the queen my daughter forever ignorant, and to raise this child myself.

Or tonight I must summon my messenger and send him to her, letting her know that elvish name of which my father was so proud.

BLOOD
AND BONE

I passed my earliest years in pygmy land. I could never ascertain how this came to happen. In all our history, there is no record that any other human being has had sustained contact with the little creatures, although we have many legends and fairy tales of human babies being stolen away and pygmy changelings left in their place. I can come on no suggestion of present-day fact behind the stories, and in my own experience the exchange theory makes no sense. Feeling as we do, both sides, who would ever consider such a thing? But then, how can one explain me?

Perhaps my mother was a venturesome woman and she ventured too far. If her time was close and birth pangs came upon her in their territory, she could not possibly have scaled the vast, sheer cliff that separates our land from theirs.

Perhaps she died naturally in giving birth to me. This is the kindest tale. Other possibilities swim through my mind in the dark reaches of the night.

What horrors might a band of pygmy hunters have wrought if they had come upon a woman groaning and helpless in her travail? But if the pygmies killed her, why did they not kill me too? My pygmy family never talked of how I came there in the years I lived with them, nor have I ever been able to find any trace of a woman missing from my own people who might have been my mother.

Through my early life with them, I came to know that the pygmies do have speech. They do communicate with each other. Their voices are very high-pitched, compared to ours, and their speech is extremely rapid. They sound like twittering birds in springtime, and my people see them as another kind of animal, fit for whatever need we may have of them. I was taken in a raid when I was five and brought to my own country. My pygmy family was killed and used, according to custom and need. My captors did not let me watch, knowing that such sights are not for children.

My new family was kind in an absentminded sort of way. I never wanted for clothes and food. I would have a bedtime story and a good-night kiss from one or another of them. They never wished to hear about my early life, however. I remember trying to tell my mother in that family about the pygmy school. "There is a difference between using your imagination and telling lies, Maveria," she said severely. "Enough of this nonsense. I don't want to hear another word."

I wanted to tell Mother about my early life. School had been horrible. I wanted her to know that even the biggest desk was tiny for me, that my knees were jammed under the ledge and usually full of splinters, that my head would bang against the lintel every time I forgot to duck, that the tricycles and the wagons collapsed under my weight and the pencils vanished in my hands. How could my fat fingers turn the pages in the tiny books? I wanted Mother to put her arms around me and hold me and tell me how awful it must have been.

Outside, nobody could play teeter-totter with me. Even if three pygmies got on the other end, I stayed on the ground. They liked to play blindman's buff, so long as I was the blind one, sawing the air with my huge, clumsy arms. "Fatty, fatty, two by four," they yelled at me, and then Sammy changed it: "Fatty, fatty, four by eight, couldn't get through the garden gate." They liked that, and chanted it at me whenever the teacher was somewhere else.

The teacher didn't like me either. I realized long afterward that it must have been scary for her to have a young child to teach who was bigger than she was. It's not really surprising that she made me sit on the floor a lot. She had one pencil that I could hold properly. On the side of it was written "Giant Pencil." I took it everywhere. I mourned it for months after it broke under my clumsy foot.

My adoptive mother would not listen. Could not, I came to understand. Five of her children had died of the bone disease. She didn't listen to the good things about my early life either. She was certain pygmy mothers could not sing. How was it possible that my mother sang lullabies to me? As for pygmy fathers, she had it on good authority that many of them ate their young.

My life among my own people has been uneventful. When I was an adolescent here, many others my age were already in the late stage of the bone disease, Sarrow's deficiency they call it nowadays. I was twenty when the chemist Sarrow found the means of keeping death at bay—even into old age, provided the medication is continued.

Fortunately I have escaped the curse of Sarrow's disease. It's almost impossible to manufacture the medicine these days. As the numbers of pygmies decline and those who remain move ever farther back from the bottom of the cliff, it becomes more difficult to procure the crucial ingredient. Pygmies are an obsession with my husband. He thinks he smells them everywhere. I suppose I might be the same if my life depended on it. He's a rare one for studying bone conditions, my husband, blood and bone. "You're a baker, not a scientist," I tell him. "Leave research to the people who are trained to do it."

Sard is a volunteer firefighter. He makes wooden toys to give to all the town children at the Great Festival. Once a week he bakes extra bread—ordinary bread—for the poor. He never forgets my birthday, or the anniversary of the day we wed. I am not married to an ogre, after all.

"Maveria, my girl," he tells me, "nobody knows as much about me as I do. I've got lots of bone. Lots of bone for things to go wrong. I need a lot of my special bread, and that's for sure." He had developed his recipe for bread long before the regular medication became so hard to get. Everybody with a Sarrow person in the family began to stockpile it, so even when any came into the pharmacy, it vanished within the hour. Most people don't even know what the special ingredient is, let alone how to use it to treat their condition.

My husband knows. There is bonemeal in his special bread. I have only ever tasted a mouthful or two. My life does not depend on it. But it tastes delicious, nothing chalky or gritty about it at all. I was sure he used cattle bones, or sheep bones, until the night I found the teeth. A big bagful of teeth, pearly little ones, some of them with the root mostly dissolved away, almost ready to come out, but a lot of them complete, root and all. Tiny teeth, like the ones my pygmy brother put under his pillow for the tooth fairy to give him money. In my country, we do not play that game.

I thought about little creatures, pygmy creatures. I thought about the rhyme my husband sometimes says. "Just my baking chant, Maveria my dear," he tells me, and chuckles. I have not asked him about the teeth. I do not want to know more than I know already.

I watch out, though. We don't have raiding parties anymore. Too many people have been killed on the cliff. Besides, there's nothing left to raid down there. But if my people can climb down, I have always realized that a pygmy can likely climb up. All the same, no matter how much you think a thing could happen, it may still be a huge surprise when it does.

I could hardly believe it when I heard the little scrittering noise at the door! It took me a while to realize where it was coming from. How strange to hear him talk, that twittering like a bird's. I was sure I had forgotten the language, but they say you never forget what you learn as a child. True or not, it all came back to me. What a talk we had!

I forgot totally about making dinner. I hadn't even stoked up my great range when I heard my husband's heavy steps. It was a bad time. Bonemeal was low, and Sard was worried. His energy was down a bit, though the disease was not yet showing any effect. But Sard had been cutting down on his bread to make the supply last, and he was liable to explode with rage, even with no provocation at all.

I plunked the pygmy youngster in the cold oven and told him not to let out a yap if he valued his life. I'm not sure he believed me, but there wasn't a squeak out of him when I shut the door.

Sard was in a joking mood. "I smell pygmy blood," he kept saying, sniffing around and opening cupboards while I cut cold meat and made salad for our meal. It must just have been coincidence—he never went near the oven—but it worried me. After dinner he settled down in front of the Holo with a six-pack, as he so often does these days. We collected gold pieces for a year to get the hologram set, the most expensive on the market. Every now and again I forget they're not really in my living room and start to talk to one of them, the Holo people; it's a good way not to have to think too much. Sard falls asleep there nearly every night.

With the oven door still closed, I cleaned up the kitchen and peeked into the living room. Noisy. Blaring set, snoring husband. I opened the oven and told the pygmy to run like blazes.

"Gotta pee," he squeaked. I'd never thought about that! He tore off toward our bedroom, and I let him go, figuring he'd find what he needed. We have a stool in there for me to reach the high cupboards, good enough for him to stand on. I hoped he had enough sense to be quiet.

He came out with a bulge under his jacket, but I never thought anything of it, just shoved him down the stairs. "You be careful down that cliff," I told him, "it's getting dark."

Next thing I heard was the beep from the living room. Sard came awake like a grampus, huffing and snorting, and took off, yelling as he went. "Some damn thief has stolen my Runman," he growled as he went by. His special Runman, with the two-way beeper that set off a signal on his belt every time the playback machine was moved! I could hear him plunging around, but in the dark he did not catch even a glimpse of the thief.

"How the hell did anybody get by you, Maveria?" He shook me a little and made a fist, just to emphasize his point.

"I don't know, dear," said I, and kept on with my mending. The more worked up Sard gets, the more calm and quiet I become. It's the only way. Eventually we went to bed. The doctors tell people like Sard to keep calm and wait. Throughout the land, scientists are doing their utmost to find a cure or even to synthesize the stabilizing medication.

It must be hell for Sard. It's bad enough for me. He was such a joyful person when I married him. We used to dance all night. Not much joy these days. We went to another funeral last week.

"I was fifteen when Evad was born," Sard told me. "They're dying younger all the time." I myself do not approve of open coffins, especially when it's Sarrow's disease. Sard, however, insisted on going up, and propelled me with a hand of iron. Short of starting a fight in the Death Palace, I could do nothing.

Evad was fallen in, almost two-dimensional. I know that's how they get, their bones just dissolve away, but it was a shock to see it, just the same. Sard caught my sideways look. "Not yet, Maveria love," he said. "Not my time just yet."

People are beginning to talk, though, and there are strange looks. They know Sard has the disease, yet it has not ravaged him. The officials are planning to search homes and confiscate hidden stores of the medication. We don't have any, of course, but Sard has put his little bit of bonemeal under the big flour sack. It should be secure enough for the moment.

I hurt his hurt, I fear his fear as the others waste away and die.

The stabilizing medicine has to be kept cold, so the officials could only search for something under refrigeration. But Sard's excellent health is a giveaway. He has taken to going to the bakery at dawn and returning either very early or after every sensible person has gone to bed.

Just the same, this healthy man is a dead man soon unless he gets more bonemeal. In the past I have heard his mill grinding. It sounds like any other machinery, a motor running, a buzz, the occasional slowdown as it works on something large, the sudden sharp snap like a shot, and the settled buzz again. He has learned to run the mill at night, when he thinks I am sleeping.

He does this out of delicacy. Yes, this big grouchy man has tremendous delicacy and sensitivity. He knows I was a child in their country, in their homeland. He has wiped the nightmare sweat from my face when my dreams re-create my pygmy family's end. For a while I dreamed often about cutting the flesh from their dead arms and legs, the yellow bone still bearing bits of clinging gristle and bloody flesh.

I can't stand to think this thought, but the knowledge has wormed its way into my mind. Sard must have caught, killed, and ground at least five pygmies in the twenty years of our marriage. There has always been enough bonemeal. One tablespoon to five loaves of bread, that's all it takes, but he must have it, one slice three times a day, four times in the winter, when cold thickens the blood.

Sard and I feel differently about the pygmies. "I know you tell me they can talk to each other, and to you," he tells me, "but I don't believe it myself. Animals, that's all they are, two-legged animals like apes, and they keep me alive, Maveria, they keep me alive."

But none of them has come his way for too long now, and I hid the one who did come. How many years of life would his bones have given Sard? I talked like a friend to the little babbling thing. He told me about his mother, who is poor; I suppose that's why he stole the Runman, though nobody in their land could possibly run with it the way we do, puny little things. It would be like cutting his throat myself, giving him to Sard.

Sard has taken to prowling the cliff top, sniffing and mumbling his little chant, though he has not found any blood to smell. We have never talked much about it. After all these years, we know each other so well.

Early in our marriage, Sard was still experimenting with different kinds of bonemeal. "How about our own bones?" I asked. "Bones from healthy people, of course, not ones with the disease."

"Our own!" He nearly jumped at me, he was so shocked. "Our own! That would be cannibalism. Pygmies, now, they're nasty puling little animals, good for bonemeal and that's all. But people! What do you think I am?"

"How about dead people, from the graveyard?" I asked. "I know it's awful, Sard, but if it would save lives? Other people's lives too, not just yours."

"It was tried," Sard said finally in a low voice. "I got all the experimental stuff. Animal bones of all kinds. Dead people. Even live people, the scientists had a few bits and pieces from accidents, as good as fresh-killed.

"Pygmy bonemeal, it's the only thing that works. It works in the stabilizing medicine, but you have to keep it cold. It works better in my bread, but I haven't told anybody else about that, and not about to either, and don't you. Who knows what would happen to me?"

Living like this makes a person think strange thoughts. If it helped him, would I give Sard an arm? In one of the old stories, a queen told Death that she would go with him and let her husband live. Her husband agreed!

Sard would never consent to let me die to save his life. I could get along without my left arm. But it wouldn't save his life. It would not even help him to live longer unless he can figure out a process that works. Maybe I can do more for him if I keep my arm. If he runs out of meal, I'll need two arms to nurse him.

I think sometimes of what will happen when the bonemeal is gone. In my thoughts, I can get through the illness. Painfully, with horror, but I know what that would be like. I can get to the Death Palace, with the casket closed and our wedding picture on the top. I cannot get past that. I cannot imagine life after Sard.

It was in one of our early conversations that Sard told me how to make his special bread. "In case I'm injured," he said. "In case I can't do it myself. It's ordinary enough, except the bonemeal: fine as flour, that must be, and from something on two legs, something that can make noises and think in a rudimentary kind of way. Pygmies are perfect. Young pygmies are the very best, there's the most power in young bones."

I've always remembered his words. I checked them out with the medicine man last time he passed this way. I didn't tell him much, just that I was curious about my husband's condition and the treatment for it. Bonemeal—from certain bones— in the medication. Only you can't get the medicine these days.

"Only a few Sarrows still alive anyway," said the medicine man. "They've all died out. It used to be common enough, but pygmies were easier to find in those days."

Aside from my visitor, I've never seen a pygmy since I came to my own people, except the ones in the museum, of course, the ones in the display. It's in the Primate Section, not Anthropology. It would be, of course.

The first time that idiot pygmy youngster came along, I hid him in the oven without even thinking about it.

"It's my blood pudding you're smelling," I told Sard when he came *clump-clump*ing in. He bought the story too, until the little idiot ran off with the Runman.

When he got back from the unsuccessful chase, Sard looked at me very carefully. "Did you have anything to do with this?" he asked. "I'm down to two bedspoons of bonemeal. I don't have extra energy for nonsense."

Bedspoons are big, but that's only enough for three months of bread. I don't know which made

Sard more upset, losing his Runman or losing the possibility of bones. "It could have been one of our people, the thief," I hazarded.

"Don't be ridiculous," he snapped. "You know better." I do too. We don't steal. No human being would take something that belonged to another, not even to save a life. Every gift must be freely given.

Sarrow people have such desperate problems, the state gives us considerable help. Sard and I need not depend on the bakery for our livelihood. We have a special portable terminal through which golden coins are delivered on demand. Sard has been known to entertain himself when he is feeling low by holding down the button to see how many coins it will produce before it cuts off. He got up to 2,304 on one occasion before tiring of this childish amusement.

Since the Runman vanished, he sits more often at the terminal. Sometimes he does not even bother to roll the coins that tumble out. "Think about it, Sard," I told him. "A supply of gold whenever we want it! You know we must not abuse the privilege. They can always take it away."

He looked at me, but not as if he were paying much attention. "It's going on the blink," he said, "not working all the time."

"Not surprising," said I. "We'd better make these last, and be thankful for honesty." Sard gave me a long, strange look.

I never expected that pygmy to come back. "Dumb kid," I said. "Where d'you keep your brains?" We never had children, Sard and I. How could anybody? With a Sarrow parent, most of them are born with the deficiency. We had two abortions, early on. After the second one, Sard had a vasectomy.

But I have a soft spot for little things. I liked this saucy brat. I even thought I'd like to cuddle the little creature like a baby and feed him a bottle. I love to hold a baby and feed it, and there is not much chance. I picked him up, but he gave me a terrific kick in the belly.

"Giantess dear," he said. I had to ask him to speak up before I could hear. They're such sloppy speakers these days, don't say anything clearly. Enunciation, that's the thing, that's what we learned at school. "Giantess dear," he yelled, and again that was the start of it and we talked and talked, an hour, two, three, and suddenly again the house began to shake like always when Sard is almost home.

"Hide!" I yelled at Jack (what an uncouth name), and I stepped up to the counter and threw the milk out of that bottle. What would Sard think if he saw that? He's not dumb, he'd notice right away.

Jack had got himself out of sight when Sard came through the door. I was afraid to light the stove, in case he'd climbed into the big oven, but Sard had brought home fresh bread, and he lit the kindling himself. He always likes hot bread. He looked surprised when I opened the door for a peek, but Jack was not there.

I saw no more of him. He must have got away in the night. In the morning, Sard's howl of rage shook the house. "Our gold terminal! Our terminal!" he roared. "What creature has been in our house? The terminal, the terminal is gone!" When Sard is exceedingly angry, he loses sight of me as a person. "Woman," he said, "you must have known."

"Not I, husband," I replied, but it is obvious he does not trust me as he used to do.

He is right too. I am not to be trusted. What a dreadful thought. I! They never asked me to swear to a promise. Everybody knew I always do what I say when I say it. Life used to be simpler.

We are getting poor fast without the terminal. Sard needs special supplements in addition to his bread. It's costly. We have also had the worst of official bureaucracy to deal with over our loss. "Never seen a case like it," mumbled the chief of police. "Are you sure you don't know anything, Maveria? I'm beginning to wonder if your early years corrupted you."

There's another problem about the terminal. I had thought it would be simple enough for them to cut off its capacity to churn out gold coins. Apparently it is not simple. The supply can be diminished. The terminal may be persuaded to act erratically. In its physical absence, however, it cannot be completely disconnected. Wherever that wretched pygmy child has taken it, it is producing gold for him and his mother. They are not poor anymore. The thought is not comforting to me.

Sard does not bake much bread these days. He has so little bonemeal for his own needs. It would be discouraging in the extreme for him to be spending his depleted energy in a bakery.

Instead he has taken to supplementing our meager income with his harp. He takes it daily into the city and makes it sing to people in need, people who are tired and fearful, people who are sad. It's a magnificent harp, but it is informed by the loving sensitivity and by the passion of the man whose fingers move on the strings.

My days have become lonely. It appears I have been waiting for him to come again. Jack. "Third time's lucky," I say. "Maybe this time you'll stay."

"For a while, giantess dear," he says, and smiles.

"Metal-mouth," say I. "That's a surprise, considering the cost of orthodontics these days."

"We've come into money, my mum and I," says Jack.

"Ah," say I. I do not say anything about *my* money. Pygmy or human, children should get their teeth fixed. My teeth are every which way, and Sard knocked out one of my lower front teeth one night. It was an accident, he doesn't know his own strength, but it wouldn't have happened if he hadn't gone through the whole of his six-pack and most of another besides. He had burned his own special bread that day, and was in a genuinely foul mood. Sard's teeth are even worse than mine.

I knew we were out of bonemeal, or nearly. Sard has been grinding up bones of sheep, cattle, horses even. "It can't hurt and may help," he says. But it isn't helping so you can notice. "It's better than nothing by a shave and a whisker, that's all," my husband says. He is getting weaker, droopy. I can see it from day to day.

He keeps trying.

Sitting here, I find myself looking thoughtfully at Jack. His bones would give Sard years and years of life. His bones.

Jack prattles on. "We've got a new cottage at the bottom of the cliff, Mum and me," he says. "I have buried a lot of the gold, and made a special bag to take the rest of it gradually to town. I've got a bank and a banker now," he laughs.

I do not laugh. I have no energy except to sit. Jack climbs up to make us a cup of coffee. "Brighten you up," he laughs.

"Okay," say I. "Here's to you." I lift my coffee mug.

I have been coming toward this decision always, ever since the pygmy children laughed at me in school. I do not hate them. I do not even despise them anymore, but they owe me. I wasn't fat, just a lot bigger, even then.

I know I have to decide three or four hours before Sard comes home. "Your mum would miss you if you never went home," I say.

"Betcher life," exclaims Jack cheerfully. "What's *that* statement in aid of?"

"Nothing," I reply. But I cannot count on him to come again.

Him or me. Him or me.

I go to the bedroom and take out my bottle of capsules and tablets. I've been saving them, never certain until now why I needed close at hand the means of painless death. Medicine men and women are so careful these days, and the pharmacies are all computerized. You can't get duplicate prescriptions like in the old days. It's taken me years to save this lot from Sard's painkillers, one and two at a time.

"Take the little harp," I say. "It has such a glorious tone, it seems almost to play your chosen melody all by itself. Many a night it has brought me sleep and magic dreams."

Jack's fingers stray to the strings. "How can you bear to be without it?" he asks.

"Easily enough," I reply. "It's time." I am starting to feel drowsy. "Take it and go," I say, more urgently.

Jack just stands there looking at me. I guess the muscles are already starting to slacken, even in my face.

In the silence we hear Sard's steps. He is a long way off, but he's a big man, my husband.

Jack takes the harp and runs. I am feeling very light. In a little while I will float. There is a letter from me for Sard, a big letter on the table. I've moved the table near the door. He can't fail to see it the instant he comes in. Killing Jack would provide bonemeal for a year or two, but it wouldn't solve my problem. Part of my mother's mystery has been explained. I've been grappling with the knowledge for more than a month. Even I have trouble accepting it. Unnatural images haunt me. Sard is sunken far in his own problems, or he would have noticed. A dozen times I've started to tell him and my mouth has closed on the words.

33

I've had my own bones tested, and I'm only half human, though I am fully human size. I am half pygmy myself: a freak.

The medicine people who did the testing are becoming more insistent: they want more bone samples to do more experiments. They want me to move to their facility. "Your best move is to work with us," says the chief. "I can tell you, the minister of health thinks you are an abomination. His view is that you should be killed and used, according to custom, and the sooner the better. 'She can't look human,' he says. 'She's not human and we know it.'"

I can't see much to choose between them. The minister wants my bones all at once. The medicine people want me in little bits.

Either way, the happy years of my life with Sard are over. My bones aren't quite as powerful as young Jack's, but they are three or four times as big. They work in the official medicine; therefore, they will also work in Sard's bread. I have figured it out very carefully. I can't save everybody, but I can give Sard a good ten years. The new bonemeal will be perfectly fresh. All Sard has to do is come in.

But what do I hear? Faintly, faintly, I hear the harp. Fool! Could the pygmy not wait to make it sing? Will Sard hear it too? Will he go tearing after Jack and never come in at all? I am imprisoned in this chair as if my limbs were held down by chains. I try to lift my little finger; it is a ton of rock.

Why have I done this? It's silly for women to sacrifice themselves. I can't bear waste. My eyes fasten on my great stove, my pride. The nickel plating glows. The black pipe has been freshly blacked. There is not a speck, not a spatter on the cream and green enamel, or the great black top. Is that my epitaph? "She kept her stove clean." Not what I had in mind. So many have died of Sarrow's. If Sard lives for another ten years because of me, that's ten more years for someone to find a cure.

I want them both to be all right. Sard and Jack. Me too, but that's not on today's menu.

I hear the harp still, faintly, faintly. Do I hear a crashing sound? Has Sard gone over the cliff? Oh, what is happening? I cannot bear not to know.

A BED
OF PEAS

What are the special properties of sand?
It shifts, moves out from under you. With sand there is no stability, no permanence. Things are not what they appear to be.

Sand insinuates itself everywhere. It slips in, grain by gritty grain. In calm weather, you live with it under your fingernails, in your pubic hair. When the dry wind rises, sand beats on your every door, into nostrils, under eyelids. The woman's dress of old Islam was created as a desperate defense against the invasion of sand, not the lascivious eyes of men.

In sandy places the habit of silence develops early. Its alternative is a mouth forever full of grit. Those who cannot, will not, learn to be silent pay for their chatter with early loss of their worn-down teeth.

I did not know the desert until well past my youth, but Hassan, my husband, was formed by it. I thought I understood the man I married. In truth, I knew the real Hassan not at all.

Our love was silent from the start. So it had to be.

36

I, who longed to publish my joy to every person at
my father's court, to command my love to be sung
in trumpets and rung in bells from every steeple,
had to content myself with whispering it to the
birds in my private garden, where Hassan would
come before dawn to the little postern gate.

The new-oiled lock yielded to the golden key I
gave him, and I would rise in the sweet air and
tiptoe over my sleeping companions to descend the
narrow stone steps to him, waiting with joyous patience at the door below.

By our own vows, Hassan the slave, Hassan the
gardener, and I the princess were husband and wife.
My father, however, continued to plot a "good" marriage for me, his only child. I found objections to all
his candidates: this one too fat, that too short; too
dumb, too talkative; too handsome, too ugly; too
young, too old.

"Daughter, do you think to remain unwed?" he
asked at last. "You have tried my patience too far.
The husband you long for is surely no creature of
this earth. I have brought before you many fine
men. Tell me now which of them best pleases you."

"Give me tonight, Father," I countered. "Let me
lie on my pillows of lavender silk and consider this
matter. Tomorrow you shall hear."

By the morrow, Hassan and I were fleeing for our
very lives. My father was a prince, but Hassan's was
a Bedouin chieftain of the desert, as powerful as any
prince and full as proud. The vagaries of conquest
and enslavement made no difference to my husband's nobility of spirit. We were well matched.

However, I had been trained from infancy to know that my marriage would be a state affair decided by my father, with advice from his council only if he chose.

Without my faithful serving woman, I might never have dreamed of challenging my fate. She sang to me the great stories, the mysteries of love: of Paris and fair Helena, for whose body the walls of Troy shivered and fell; of Eurydice and Orpheus, who followed her through the gates of hell and by his love and his music won her release; of dark Pluto, who stole Persephone into a living grave— and all for love.

I listened and believed. Hassan and I spoke with our eyes, our fingers, long before words came to our tongues, long before the first syllable escaped.

The flames of my father's rage would explode into a million sparks when he learned that I had run off with Hassan, and that we had escaped on his own charger, an Arabian without peer, which could carry double all night and still outstrip every other horse in the royal stables.

My beloved Hassan and my father's great steed could have continued our headlong flight forever, it seemed. I betrayed us. I, or more accurately, more kindly, my body, princess-soft. An old story tells of the princess who felt a pea through twenty mattresses. Foolish people tell it in her praise. Nonsense! What benefit can it be? Such sensitivity makes woman or man unfit for life, except as a pampered pet.

But such was I.

In the beginning of our flight, I held my arms around Hassan and molded myself to his dear back, nuzzling out angles in his bone and muscle I had not tasted before. My body clung with his to the broad saddle, felt with his the jolt of every landing of those great equine hoofs.

How quickly the ecstasy passed. How soon each burst of pleasure turned to pain!

Hassan felt my trouble almost at the instant that my numb hands lost their grip. His own arm of steel held me while without a word he brought our steed to a halt. In minutes we were in full career again, my half-swooning self now tied to Hassan in front, cushioned by the soft leather satchel in which I'd packed a few clothes, mostly stolen from my women. Nothing of my own suited our flight or a future life in the desert sands.

But our journey at that time stopped many a league short of the desert. Hassan saw quickly how unfit I was either for sustained travel or for sustained life in tents and sand. He kept his silence, but carried me and revised our plans as he rode.

He sold our charger a day later to a traveler in the next kingdom. Tenderly he kissed away my tears of grief. "Weep, my love," he told me. "I well recall my feelings when I was ravished away from my people, from every thing and every person I held dear." I had not known any man could be so gentle or so kind. How different from my father!

My bruises, alas, were not to be kissed away. They rose, purple and blue, from the upper surfaces of both my feet to my left cheek, which had lain

39

against his water flask as he held me in that wild gallop. We continued our journey on a peasant's hay cart for three days more, Hassan's unspoken plan to throw my father's people off our scent.

A little mountain town was our refuge. Hassan's own loving hands bathed my body, lessening a little the stiffness in every aching joint. Hassan's rough hands kneaded warm oil into my skin. We could both see that he would do well to care for a soldier wounded in battle, but that his strong, rough hands abraded my princess skin as much as they healed it. Hassan found the little house and the woman to tend it and me.

Our own home. Our little garden was shaded by the massive stone wall that guarded the great house next door, but we were able to grow sweet-smelling herbs: thyme, basil, rosemary; and the pansies throve. From our upper window, I could see our neighbor's kitchen garden and her gardener's bent back as he went up and down the rows.

Sometimes I would see the lady's coach drive out, four jet-black horses stepping high and proud. I never met Lady Grendel, never saw her. She sat far back in the coach. Kitchen gardens, no doubt, were not worth her notice. When I was a princess, I never knew there was such a place as a kitchen garden. Maybe Lady Grendel was no different from me.

Who could have thought that Hassan and I would live in that tiny cottage for the next twelve years?

I healed slowly when we first came there, hardened more slowly still. But I did harden. Hassan became a trader in horses. His Bedouin canniness and expertise earned us a living. The sale of the great charger provided funds for his first purchases. Our town, however, was small and remote from the travel routes. Its remoteness helped to keep us safe from pursuit but hindered our gaining more than a subsistence through Hassan's efforts, however valiant.

My help was also needed. The market for fine embroideries such as I could execute was limited. My energy was limited likewise, although I was skillful with my needles and my silks. Slowly the word spread and the wealthy women from neighboring estates and towns paid an excellent price for all that I could do.

And thus we lived, quiet and contented enough. If Hassan ever longed for his people and his tents, if he hated the cold mountain rains, he never spoke those thoughts.

I would have liked a baby, but Hassan smiled and shook his head. "Truly?" I asked. "My father always wanted sons."

I could feel my husband eyeing my slender body. "You're no breeding mare, sweet love," he said. We talked less and less of our childlessness and might have lived out our lives in that quiet place.

After eleven childless years, however, I conceived.

Ah, how I welcomed the daily struggle with nausea, lost again each day, the strange sweet ache in my breasts, the drop of clear fluid that I could squeeze from my nipple.

Hassan gave up his horse-trading trips and stayed with me. I stopped making clothes for other babies and created tiny, exquisite garments for my own, falling asleep often in midstitch. The princess body still asserted itself, though it was less debilitating than before. Certain foods, however, I craved with single-minded ferocity.

Lady Grendel's lettuce! I could see the bright green rows from my bedroom window, with the gardener plucking the occasional upstart weed from the rich black soil. I longed for those lettuces. Platefuls, pailfuls of lettuce to quiet my rapacious mouth.

Hassan bought lettuces in the market. Lady Grendel's thick rows mocked me, and I vomited what Hassan had bought.

My husband spoke to the gardener, who spoke to the housekeeper, who went to Lady Grendel. Hassan was summoned to explain my craving for her lettuce. The next day three feet of ice-green succulence was cut and washed and brought to me. I ate every bit, along with three thick slices of hard white bread and goat's-milk cheese from our own goats.

"I don't care for that Lady Grendel," Hassan told me. "She enjoys power over other people altogether too much. In the town, they say she's a witch. Let her keep her spells away from us, that's all I can say." Had my husband ever made so long a speech before? Not in my experience, and I had learned to trust him about people as much as I did about horses.

"I've had my fill of her lettuce," I responded. "I'll not send you to her again."

Misplaced confidence. The following week my

yearning for that lettuce was stronger than before. Again Hassan went to Lady Grendel, and a bargain was struck. This time Hassan could cut lettuce for me for a week, as much as I wanted. The rest of the first green row vanished into my maw, and half of the middle row. Lady Grendel vociferously deplored her bargain to everyone within hearing. When after a week my craving resounded more loudly than ever, a restless obbligato in my mouth and stomach, she would not be moved.

"The rest is for me," she declared. "You've had all you're going to get."

This time Hassan scoured the countryside for lettuce to please me. He bought lettuce from the high mountains and lettuce from the lush valleys, lettuce grown in clear sunlight and lettuce darkened by shade, all of it exquisitely fresh, brought to me new-picked, with the night dew still crisping its leaves.

None of it lessened my craving. I sat at my bedroom window for hours on end, brooding over the row and a half of giant emeralds that lay twelve feet or so below. Obsessed with dreams of lettuce, I refused all other food. Hassan shook his head at the princess, me. I had seen my husband act tenderly. Now, had I noticed, he became quietly frantic. I starved. Over and over I saw myself jumping from my window, sinking into the soft black earth, crunching the crisp green. How hard it was not to make that plunge!

Hassan sat beside me for three long days. With hands and breaking voice he tried to coax me back to myself. Then he went to Lady Grendel and made his bargain for my life. I have long since been sure that she planned the whole abominable scheme. Her enchantments created that craving. There is no wickedness so great that that lady would not contemplate it. And after thought comes action. She would test her power.

It was no contest.

Knowing that the rest of the lettuce was mine, but that no more of it existed when this was gone, I controlled myself. I ate that green wonder like a child with a birthday cake who keeps the icing till last and then eats it crumb by sugary crumb.

The time when the child should have been born came and went. I pushed my gigantic belly sluggishly around the house. Lady Grendel sent her physician, who administered a noxious dose and broke my water. "Get out," Hassan ordered him, and sent our serving woman for the midwife.

Then all Hassan's concerns about my useless princess body were justified. No breeding mare, indeed. My muscles contracted and expanded in mind-numbing spasms, but after a day and a night I was not delivered. Slowly I came to understand that this agony would continue forever, that the baby must be dead or would surely die, that I would die myself. My prayer was "Let it be over. Over. Now."

In the end the midwife took my husband aside. "I can do nothing more," she told him, wiping her tears. "A doctor might cut the child in pieces from her body and save her life. Otherwise she will surely die."

Lady Grendel was waiting for Hassan's appeal. Her whey-faced physician manipulated my body and delivered my child. A daughter, but they could not rouse me by then to tell me so. "She may live," said the doctor. "The child also. I cannot tell. She must have rest and care at all times of day and night."

"The child is mine, and I will care for her," said Lady Grendel. "One of my women has recently given birth. She has milk for half a dozen infants."

I wondered later if Hassan even noticed when they left, Lady Grendel and her accomplice, and our child. I never held my baby, never kissed the tiny hands and feet. I knew nothing at all, not that night and not for the next delirious month, after which it seemed I likely would survive after all. By that time Lady Grendel had packed up house and household and departed with her entourage, destination unknown.

Slowly I came alive and began to understand that my baby was gone, my baby, my child. Long before understanding was complete, I retreated into madness. I wrapped a brick in the silk shawl I had so lovingly embroidered and would cradle it in my arms and rock my days away. Hassan I no longer recognized—would not face him, even, turning away or hiding my features beneath tousled, graying hair: I, who had prided myself on my coronet of golden braids.

"I wanted to give up too," Hassan told me, years later. "It would have been so easy. I could not bear to look at you, and I could not bear you to be out of my sight. I had only to approach and you would scream. You would hide your brick baby, shielding it with your body—from me. And you were right. It was as if you knew how I had betrayed you. I could not bring you food or drink. I could not comb the knots from your hair. Anybody else, but not me who loved you more than my life."

My poor Hassan! But he was a chieftain's son; he would not give up.

My hands, skilled in creation, now proved equally skilled in destruction. My embroidery scissors reduced the exquisite baby wardrobe to scraps of silk. After that my attendants hid scissors, needles, and knives and gave me rough fabric to tear. It yielded quickly enough to my fingers and teeth. When the cloth was shredded, I bit and tore my own flesh. My former clients, in pity, sent their discarded garments, which I shredded mechanically, day after unchanging day.

Hassan had hired a second woman, so that one would always be awake and watching me. Now he went off on long horse-trading trips. At the end of a year he was ready. Again he tied me in front of him on his horse. Again he cushioned me with the leather satchel, full this time of different clothes.

"Now we will find our baby," he told me. "However long it takes. We will find her and get her back."

Somewhere I heard and attended. Or perhaps I was too numb to feel or understand at all. I made no struggle, then or later. My body remembered another time when I had been carried thus. I felt myself comforted. Held close against Hassan's loving body, I began to heal. So, he told me later, so did he.

Now was our time in the desert, for he had heard that Lady Grendel had gone that way. I started learning to live with sand. Hassan did not find the lady, but in the search he found his father's tents again.

I began dimly to comprehend what he had given up on my account all those years before. His father no longer rode. The ancient man was carried in a litter. He knew Hassan, however, and made a great welcome for him.

"I thank you, my father, more than these words can express," said Hassan, "but I will not take my place as your eldest son. I have been gone too long. My brother has that place. Besides, I and my wife must continue our quest. We seek our only daughter, my father, and will never be at peace until she is found."

"Yet take a place in our councils," said his father. "You would honor yourself and me. We will send messengers to find this Lady Grendel who stole your daughter. The desert has its own network. Our messages will spread. She might change her name and her way of living, but sooner or later, we will hear of her. Then you can be on your way with fighting men to take back your own."

"Brave words, Father," Hassan said with a smile. "I accept your help. Indeed, why else am I here? Your messengers will find her quicker than I could. Until that day, I will ride with you and our people."

Me too they welcomed. In the desert water is as

precious as diamonds, but the women washed me and massaged my skin with delicate oils. They enveloped me in love and their own clothing, doing battle with my terrors and with the omnipresent sand. For the life of their animals and their people, the tribe had to keep on the move, making their seasonal journey to the south and then turning gradually northward again. For my sake, they stayed longer in one place at the beginning, and moved more slowly that year.

When did I come to myself enough to challenge Hassan? I looked at him one day and knew. "You did it," I said flatly. "You gave our unborn baby for that lettuce, didn't you. That was why you never sent to get her back. There were other women who could have nursed her, not in that witch's house."

Then it was well for Hassan that he had his father, his brothers, his tribe. He had little enough of me. I was filled with horror at the sight of him, the father who had bargained away our child.

"What choice had I?" he spat at me one day. "One way I lost you both to certain death. The other I lost one for certain, whether to death or Lady Grendel, who then could say?" Then, in the most sorrowful voice I have ever heard, he added, "But I have lost you both, just the same. I have lost you both."

I thought but did not say, Better I had died. Better we both had died than to live so betrayed. But Hassan's sorrow had opened the gates of my heart. When I could truly see what he had done, how could I not venerate this man who could face so hard a choice? He loved our child as I did; he had lost her as much as I. "I am alive because of you," I told him. "It is in my own power to cease to regret that it is so."

In the blowing desert sand I finally lost forever the useless princess body. Now I rode my own horse. My softness turned to muscle; jelly became steel. "When we pursue Lady Grendel," I told Hassan, "I shall ride beside you."

We both knew we would get news of her one day, however long it might take. Sometimes one or the other of us lost patience, but mostly we stayed quiescent, waiting. Nobody thought it would be yet another twelve years.

Each year we celebrated our daughter's birthday. Now she was two years old, now five, now—how could it be?—ten. Each time we invited all the children of her age to the banquet. We watched them jealously. Afterward we made up our stories. Often she would be more beautiful, more clever, wiser, gentler, and tougher than all the others put together. Occasionally we fantasized a flaw in her perfection—a squint? a mole? a temper?—for protection against the day when we would truly hold her in our arms.

At length came news to take us on our way, though we were uncertain whether this was indeed the trail of the woman we sought. A rich woman had come to the city at the edge of the desert with her household and "her" baby at the right time. She had stayed for several years, building a large walled house. We thrilled and shuddered to hear the child's name: Letitia. The "mother's" name was different, but we had always expected that.

All stories told of the child's great beauty, her charm and wit.

After a few years, however, the mistress had sold her property again and moved, taking only two of her original servants with her, a man who had to be either the whey-faced physician or his brother, and a woman who was her housekeeper and willing slave.

This time our inquiry moved beyond the desert. As names and locations began to reach us, Hassan and I set forth to take our own place in the search at last. The bravest men of the tribe vied for places in our train, including Hassan's four brothers. "This is not the time, my brothers and my friends," Hassan decided finally. "We have as yet no sure news of her we seek. Two can follow a trail better than ten. This trail is sure, we feel it in our hearts, but it is cold. We two, my dear wife and I, must follow it. When we have found our daughter, we will plan well what to do and send for you if there is need."

We rode out on the two sturdiest horses, with gold and silver in our satchels and emeralds and rubies sewn into the folds of our long tan cloaks. Although we told each other again and again not to be too hopeful, our hearts beat fast as we approached the city and found the great stone-walled mansion Lady Grendel had built. Built and left again.

Three times we followed a likely trail. The first led

us to a giantess with a dwarfed and deformed son. At the end of a second trail, two years later, we found a woman with skin of gleaming ebony and a daughter full as black. "Do not forget," I said, "that Lady Grendel is an enchantress. Hassan, do you not believe she could change the shape of her face or the color of her skin?" But we talked long with the woman and at last were well convinced it was not she we sought.

It was three more years before again we felt that quickening in our hearts and muscles that told us we were once more on a warm trail. This third trail led toward a great forest. The woman who might be our quarry lived by herself on the outskirts of a city at the forest's edge. "Her daughter was as lovely as a summer day," the innkeeper's wife told us, "with shining golden hair, the longest and most lustrous I have seen. A shy maid, and gentle too. But she has not been seen these three years past. No news of her either. Her mother is rich as a queen and as well guarded. More than one young man has sought the maiden and not been seen again."

Hassan and I looked at each other, horror vying with despair. Was she dead then, after all this time? Were we to find no more of our daughter than her grave?

"We have to get closer to that house," I said.

"Yes," my husband agreed. "When we get to know some of them, we can know who might be loose-lipped, or who could perhaps be bought with a ruby. It is time for business once more. I wonder where the best horses are to be found?"

Hassan started trading again. I was fearful to let my remaining embroideries be seen, although they might have got me an easy entree to the house. Lady Grendel knew my style all too well. My hands had long since become too hard and coarse to do new work with fine silks, perhaps to find a new style and new motifs. No, Hassan was our best hope. He had changed as much as I had over the years, his dark hair now winged with white. As a young man he had been clean-shaven. Now his graying beard was long. His eyes, still brilliant blue in the dark face, were his one unchanging feature. Safe or not, however, we had little choice. And after I had bribed a servant's child for a view of the Mistress, none at all. She called herself Nirana now, and had adopted the woman's dress of Islam, which hid both figure and face. Outside her own walls, she was totally concealed. Inside she discarded the chador and was revealed in gauzes and silks, glittering with gems. Unchanged were the raven hair, the dark eyes and heavy brows, the narrow mouth and pointy chin. How little she had altered. How much had I!

My muscles tensed, ready to carry me at a bound from the darkness of the serving room where I watched. My hands felt themselves grasping her throat. I could feel heat like steam rising from my body. I sat on my raging hands, stilled my raging heart. "Not yet," I muttered. "Not yet." At length I rose and let the child I had bribed lead me nervously back to the garden gate, where Hassan waited, much as he had waited at my father's court so long ago. One look at me and his smile rose again, a cruel smile that shook me with delight.

The stable master loved his long water pipe of an evening. Hassan found the local source of the finest opium and bought it. I knew how he hated the smoke, hated the daze that came with smoking. It was a father's sacrifice he made, making a crony of the man, sitting in the smoke, trying to breathe as little as possible of the cloying fumes. But he heard the stories. "Don't tell anybody. There's a tower in the forest. A tower with a window but no door. Three men built it—haven't been seen since. That was when the young mistress vanished. Went away, her mother said, sent away to school." The man laughed coarsely. "Never believed it myself. No horses for a long journey. No. She was growing up, she was." He sketched a woman's shape in the smoky air. "The men was beginning to buzz around, and Mama Mistress couldn't stand it."

"She's in the tower, then?" said Hassan, keeping the shudder from his voice.

"Where else?" replied his informant. "The old lady rides out every couple of days. Takes her woman with her sometimes, or the man who's served her all these years."

"How does anybody get in, if there's no door?"

"They don't, as I hear it. She has a rope with a bucket and hauls things up and down. I never seen it myself, but the young lad was taken out there one day when Mama Mistress was ill. He talked to me one night when he shouldn't have." The man struggled to sit upright. "I shouldn't be either. Look, I didn't say nothing, mind." In his terror the stable master knocked over his pipe, and all was forgotten as Hassan stamped out the sparks.

"That boy isn't around these days either," Hassan told me in great frustration a day or two later. "Anybody who knows anything, they all disappear."

"We must follow her into the forest," I said.

"Very carefully," Hassan agreed.

"If this is our daughter, she will be seventeen years old next month. Seventeen years old!" Lots of parents find it hard to imagine their children growing up even when they see them all the time. Was it harder for me, who had never seen my child?

Hassan and I prepared to watch for Lady Grendel and follow her. For the next two days it rained, not a gentle rain but a torrential downpour such as I had not seen since my childhood and had never experienced, protected as I had been in my princess days. Desert-dwellers are ill prepared to deal with rain. Hassan dickered for local garments to replace our sodden cloaks, and for warm woolens to wear next to our skin. Sniffling and sneezing, we waited with our horses not far from a little wooden door set into the great stone wall. If the stable master had told us right, this was the door through which the Mistress or her messenger would ride.

For two days we waited, and no one came through that door.

Could there be another exit? Might she have changed her route? "We'll give it one more day,"

Hassan decided, "then we'll separate. I'll watch this gate; you watch the front."

But that day the rain stopped and our archfoe ventured forth. Her maid led the horse through the wooden door and held the animal for Lady Grendel to mount, which she did very nimbly. She wore a peasant kirtle with her skirts kilted up, the better to ride. Panniers hung heavily from both sides of her saddle. Perhaps the story about the tower with a window but no door was true. Perhaps food and water were transported to a prisoner there.

Her path led deep into the forest. Rain still dripped from the leaves, but there were few sounds other than the *clip-clop* of my lady's gray mare. Soundlessly I gave thanks that Hassan had tied rags around our horses' feet; no sound of iron shoe on stone would ring out to give us away.

Lady Grendel rode swiftly for a city woman, but Hassan and I easily kept her in view. Gradually the path closed in, however, and became more difficult to follow. Hassan went ahead, pausing occasionally to sniff the air and listen. We were almost on top of her horse before we realized Lady Grendel had tethered her mount and must be pushing ahead on foot. At once Hassan was gentling the startled animal, speaking softly as only he could do. The horse had raised its head, but no whinny sounded.

Lady Grendel's reason for dismounting was not far to seek. Our feet squelched in swampy mud. We pushed back cedars that jumped at us and caught our clothes. Ahead we could hear the *slap-squish* of

Lady Grendel's progress. There was no way to muffle our own footsteps, although an animal would surely sound much the way we did. The footprints we followed faded as the swampy muck smoothed itself; no doubt ours would vanish as soon. Hassan led me in a half-circle whenever we could see that our footsteps might remain to betray us later. At the edge of the swamp the path was firm again, lined deep with years of pine needles, brown and dry.

It was late afternoon when we finally glimpsed a clearing. Outlined in the sunlight was the tower, built heavy and square of some dark stone that even the sunlight could not soften.

"Letitia," called the woman we followed, "Letitia, let down your hair. I've brought you food and water, my girl. I'm coming up."

No response. The clearing was still. Not even a bird sang in the fading light.

"Wake up, Letitia," came the call again, sharp and shrill. Then, "By God and the devil too, she's gone!"

Lady Grendel strode back across the meadow so fast that Hassan and I needed all our skill and training, all our superb physical conditioning, to reach our horses ahead of her and find a place where we could pull them off the path. She would have noticed immediately if she'd been noticing anything. But she was not, merely riding like a madwoman back toward town.

Hassan and I let her go and returned to the tower to see what we could find. Many times that day I had blessed my hard, tough body, but it was difficult indeed to struggle through that cedar swamp for the third time that day. Hassan too was walking slowly; I think he was glad to pause.

On the far side of the tower, a ladder lay on the ground. The grass was cropped, and droppings showed where a horse or perhaps two horses had been tethered. We leaned the ladder against the tower. It reached the sill of the one high window, and a little beyond, but not much. "You go," I muttered to Hassan. "I'm shaking too much."

"Me too," replied my husband through clenched teeth. We held each other for a long moment. Then, without a word, I began to climb. Hassan held the ladder until I had clambered inside; then he followed me. We turned to face the dwelling together.

A table and chair were placed near the window. A divan could be discerned against the opposite wall. I went forward and touched coverlets of rich silk and gossamer-fine wool. I buried my head in the soft pillows, realizing at once that my daughter might have knelt here just like me, like me wetting this very pillow with her tears.

An exclamation from Hassan brought me to his side. He was staring at the table, where a single sheet of some heavy writing material was held by a paperweight of shimmering glass. Our daughter's writing? Later I was thankful that she had that much education. Hassan and I read the page together.

"Farewell, Mother." The writing sloped and wandered. "I have found another human being, or rather, he has found me. He has brought a ladder, Mother, and he has cut off my hair. I will never let it down again."

The note was unsigned. Hassan and I looked down and saw the golden hair tumbled everywhere. Indeed, we were standing on and in it, unnoticing until now. Hassan's hand trembled violently as he lifted a lock of my hair. Faded and graying now, but once the same gold as that at our feet.

I took the letter and folded it. It was not meant for me, I knew, but it said "Mother," and I was her mother, whatever she might believe. Hassan picked up a handful of the golden hair and twisted it into a ring. He was first down the ladder, and held it again for me.

The tale of our further wanderings is quickly told. We followed them easily enough for three days, after which they vanished and we could gain no slightest trace. Hassan sent for some of his people. With their help, he arranged that Lady Grendel's saddle should come loose one day during a wild boar hunt. She was in the vanguard and fell heavily. We were never sure whether the fall killed her, or whether the galloping riders who could not swerve aside in time were needed to complete the job. Happily, she did not survive.

Hassan also activated the network that had previously brought us the news we needed to find Letitia. If it could be done once, it could be done again. It was almost a year, however, before we heard of the royal wedding that would soon be celebrated in a neighboring kingdom, of the beloved prince and his mysterious bride, who dazzled all with her halo of golden hair.

It seemed not the right moment to make ourselves known. Indeed, we wondered if the right moment would ever come, even after Hassan had become master of the royal stables and we both saw the young couple almost every day, at the beginning and at the end of their ride.

Now perhaps the moment is at hand. The princess has not ridden for several months. She awaits the birth of her first child. Yesterday, however, she came to me on her walk. She and her lady rested in my hall. They drank wine from my goblets and ate sweetmeats from my silver tray.

"I wish I could find my real parents," she said wistfully. "I'd like grandparents for the baby. I called a woman Mother, but she was not my mother, surely. No mother could have shut her child away as she did me."

Her violet eyes, the twins of my own, are troubled. Perhaps I could—perhaps tomorrow Hassan and I can—reveal ourselves at last. I would like to be a grandmother. I would like to make sure that any new little princess learns to ride as she learns to walk. No soft princess body for her. She can learn to sleep on a bed of peas.

THE VOICE
OF LOVE

Sometimes people think they know a story, but they never know the whole of it. And always, some of the details are wrong. Take the little mermaid, the quiet and pensive sea child, whose eyes were the blue of the deepest ocean and whose soft skin was translucent as a rose petal.

On her very first trip to the surface of the ocean, she watched the birthday celebration of a young and handsome human prince. She saw fireworks for the first time. She held the prince's head above the waves after his ship sank in a wild, sudden storm. She cradled his unconscious body against her own gentle breast all through the long night, keeping him from drowning while wind and waves tossed them willfully. Buffeted by the waves, she refused to sink to safety in the ocean depths.

By morning, when the waters calmed, she was exhausted and in love. She brought his limp body ashore and watched while others revived him. Her unblinking eyes memorized the woman who cradled his head in her arms, whose shining black hair fell in a screen about his face.

It was bitter sorrow for the mermaid to go back alone to her father's coral palace and her own undersea garden. Hour after hour she gazed mournfully at a white marble statue of a young man with curly hair and dimpled chin. Sometimes she thought the statue looked exactly like her prince. At other times she realized that she was forgetting his living features; she knew only the chiseled stone.

The mermaid braved a forest of deadly tentacles to find the sea witch in her underwater hut of bleached bones and ask for a spell. But the sea witch took her glorious voice as payment for transforming a mermaid's tail into two delectable female legs. The little mermaid reached her prince, and reached him in human guise. Her love, however, was silent.

As for the prince's story, who has bothered to tell it? An idiot who could neither see nor hear the one who loved him so dearly, that's the prince.

Or was it more complicated than that?

The prince had no slightest inkling that she had given up her home and her voice on his account and that on his account she walked in pain. He had no notion that he owed her his life. He never knew it was the little mermaid who had been buffeted by debris and waves as she swam to pull him clear of the wrecked ship, who had interposed her tender body between him and the rocks, who had landed him on the shore where he opened his eyes.

He had always been surrounded by affection. No wonder he saw nothing extraordinary in hers. They became inseparable companions. She was his confidante, his comforter, his friend. He wore her like an old shoe.

When his parents later imported a princess at great expense to be his bride, the prince was ready to receive her politely and to tell her he had no desire to marry, neither her nor any other. When she put a slender hand out from between the curtains of her litter, he took it with no feeling at all. Then she stepped out. The prince's face turned white, then dark red. He caught his breath. His heart pounded. Surely this was the woman who had saved his life!

That mouth so sweetly curved, those dark eyes had been only a few inches from his own when he began to revive after cheating the bitter seas. He could still feel the silk of her black hair on his face. How often he had dreamed of her! A princess too! Their wedding day was quickly set. His silent companion, so dear to him only the day before, was ousted from his mind and heart. The prince had neither time nor thought for anyone except his bride.

Day by day, always silent, the little mermaid faded. Her skin lost its hint of rose. She paled, becoming translucent as the finest marble. Maybe she finally found a soul and maybe she didn't, but blew away like sea foam. For certain, she was gone from the story forever when the sun rose the day after the royal wedding. It was not her fate to be a prince's bride.

For weeks, no thought of her crossed, even momentarily, the prince's mind. In his private suite at the great palace, he and his princess were on honeymoon. The delight of eating a piece of melon, holding it in his mouth for her to nibble, and in sweet return nibbling a strip of candied ginger from her lips, then parting them with darting tongue! And whether he tasted ginger or tasted the woman, he could not distinguish. "I love you, love you, love you," they told each other, as flesh answered flesh, young and hot and firm.

In the lulls, dovelike they murmured and cooed. Sphinxlike they lay or sat together and gazed in wonder at their own features reflected in each other's eyes. Often he sat beside her with a peacock fan, making a gentle breeze on her oval face, her slender neck, her white shoulders, her mounded breasts.

Spring, with its heavy-scented flowers, passed into languorous summer heat. "More jewels, darling" and "Another gown, my sweet" were the prince's constant litanies.

"How you spoil me, dear husband" and "How I love to be spoiled" were his wife's unfailing replies.

"Surely the goddess of love herself was your ancestress," he told her, forgetting that the goddess of love was cruel and heedless of all but herself.

Suddenly one morning the prince found himself pushing away his wife's white arms. For the first time since his wedding day, he remembered there was a world outside these rooms. He went down the ocean stair and swam far out into a cold and placid sea. It was like plunging from a steambath into an icy stream. He swam back thoughtfully.

"Tonight," he announced to his bride, "we will take our dinner in the great hall. It is time."

The princess's women dressed their mistress in a gown of red silk encrusted with crimson gems. Its high collar formed a loose band, revealing to her husband what it concealed from others less happily positioned, her long slender neck and the gentle swell of her breasts. The women rummaged in the royal coffers and brought long strands of pearls to braid into their mistress's heavy black hair.

"Not pearls," the prince commanded abruptly. "Pearls are not your gem."

A very different vision had appeared suddenly in the prince's mind. Never before had he thought of his little companion, that charming elfin creature who had spent every waking moment with him for three years, as a woman! Of all her clothes, she loved best a boy's suit of white velvet. Collar and cuffs bore a device of dolphins, picked out in the most exquisite pearls. It had been his gift to mark the second anniversary of the day she had landed so strangely at his court. With it she used to wear a snood of pearls that caught and confined the rich auburn of her shining hair.

How could he not have noticed her absence all this time? He lifted his hand to have her summoned, and then changed his mind. How strange he felt! Would it be best to meet her now as if casually? Could he wait until evening?

At dinner his eyes jumped impatiently about the room. His head throbbed with his wife's idle chatter. It seemed suddenly a blessing that his dear little friend could not speak.

But where could she be?

"Vizier," he growled, leaning across the high table.

"Highness," mumbled the vizier with his mouth full. He dropped the chicken thigh he had been munching and tried to swallow a large piece of meat without chewing it. He choked and sputtered.

The prince's fingers drummed on the table. He glared at the vizier's crimson face. "Where is she?" he demanded. "Where is my pearl girl, my companion, my little friend?"

The vizier looked around him helplessly. She was gone. That was all he knew. He said so.

"Gone, do you tell me?" thundered the prince. "At your peril do you tell me any such thing! If she is for the moment elsewhere, get her here. Immediately."

"I hear and obey," muttered the vizier. It was impossible to avoid hearing the prince, but equally impossible to obey his command. The only person who could remember seeing the missing one was the prince's little page. On the wedding night the page had been summarily banished from his bed inside the door of the prince's room. Lonely and cold, he had wandered to the stairway that led down into the sea, where he had observed the prince's dear companion sitting on the bottom stair, her legs hidden by the water. He longed to speak to her but could not force his misery on her, so continued to sit apart and watch. "Near daybreak, I must have dozed off," he said. "I shut my eyes for a second, and she was gone."

The following morning the vizier reported to his prince that his companion had gone away temporarily with a troupe of acrobats. "Acrobats?" muttered the prince, unbelieving.

"Yes indeed, Highness," lied the vizier, "she wanted to find new skills to delight you and your bride. When she has learned to her satisfaction, she will be back."

"Send for her."

"I have done so already, Highness. But she does not ride swiftly, as Your Highness knows. It may take some time."

The prince returned to his bride, whom he had left going through the caskets of his family jewels, planning new necklaces, new tiaras, new eardrops to wear with all her new costumes. With the royal jeweler, she was arranging rubies, diamonds, and pearls in an ornate design.

Again a vision of his missing little friend popped into the prince's head. Abruptly he lowered his hand, scattering the design. "Not the pearls," he muttered, "they are not your gem."

The bride wheedled and cajoled. Then screamed at him.

"Put away the jewels," he ordered the jeweler. "Another day my wife may wish a design of rubies and diamonds. Not pearls."

He turned away from his princess and went to sit on the sea stair where he had sat so often with his dear friend. Her absence was like a toothache, sometimes sharp or throbbing, sometimes dulled. How could he not have missed her before? In his mind, wife and friend stood side by side. Wife: lushly beautiful, opulently sensual. A man could drown in her body for a time, but not forever. A crow's voice when she was displeased, and a vixen's temper. Friend: full of elfin grace, merry and pensive by turns, silent always. How could he ever have looked on her silence as a flaw? She knew his every wish before he spoke, often before he had even formulated his desire in his mind. How they laughed when she sat beside him, or rode her white palfrey at his side.

Above all she loved to dance for him. Sometimes she danced like a rose blowing in a soft breeze. At other times she seemed the toy of the wild storm wind, blown like a leaf about the marble terrace. She never repeated herself exactly. Because he could not anticipate her, he was never for a moment bored.

Yet there was always a poignancy in her dancing, a look behind the smile that felt somehow as if she were dancing on sharp knives.

The prince had always planned to have the royal scribe teach her to read and write, so that he could learn her stories. Why had he delayed? He hated to be apart from her, just as she had hated any separation from him. Perhaps he had realized that pain was part of her history, and he did not altogether want to know about it. Strange thoughts for a prince!

She had been gone for three months, and he was just realizing it. The prince was little accustomed to thinking of others, yet now he could think of nothing but his friend. This was how she must have felt from the day he married, an agony in her bones. No wonder she had gone away.

More to the point, would she return? Again the vizier was sent for. "What message did you send? I want to know exactly. Where is she? How many days' travel? How many days for me, with the swiftest horse in my stable?"

The vizier hemmed and hawed. Three days away, or maybe ten or more. In the direction of the desert, no, close to the forest, infested by outlaw gangs, not safe for the prince.

"Liar!" cried the prince, as he struck his vizier a great buffet across the face. The man fell to his knees and bowed his forehead to the ground. His shoulders quivered.

"You are waiting for me to pronounce your execution," began the prince slowly. "I may—or I may not. Your life can be forfeited at my command. Now we will have the truth."

When the tale was done, he sent the man away. She had gone away herself. Nobody knew where she might be. He could send a proclamation throughout the land asking her to return, asking for news of her. She might hear, or she might not. Hearing, she might or might not come.

Only one place in the vast palace gave him any
small comfort: the sea steps from which she had
suddenly appeared—could it be no more than four
years ago? He sat there day after endless day. The
late autumn storms sent waves crashing against his
body. He shuddered and held the railing, but did not
move back. This was his birthday night re-created,
the storm night when his ship had been sunk and
he had so strangely survived.

"You didn't save me," he muttered, thinking of
his wife. "Only a sea creature could have brought
me from such a sea."

But then he remembered that his bride had never
claimed to have saved him. He sent for her. "When I
first saw you," he began, "how did I get ashore?"

"Don't think you can suddenly start talking to me
again and everything's all right," she told him icily.

"No." His smile was bitter. "Tell me, nonetheless."

"You were just there the morning after the big
storm. You were on the shore, above the tideline,
close to the temple. Your clothes were a mess—but
what was left was all velvet and silk and gold chains.
My maidens brought me to you. I've told you about
it often enough. I was sick of lessons. You were a
diversion."

"Was I conscious then?"

"No, it took you a long time to come round. We
sent for my physician. For a while we were sure
you'd die."

"Unconscious. How . . . ?"

"The doctor wondered how you got there too. He

69

said you couldn't have got yourself ashore. Later, one of my maidens said she saw a face in the seaweed, out behind a rock. Somebody, something watching both of us. I never believed her, though."

Not long after, on a clear cold moonlit night while the prince again sat alone at the sea stair, his dear friend's face, her shoulders and arms too, rose suddenly from the ocean. "You are back," he cried joyfully, ready to plunge in and gather her to his heart.

"I don't understand." The moment she spoke, he knew his error. This was not his dear one, though the resemblance was close. "I am looking for my sister. My sisters and I have risen many times, seeking our littlest one. What has become of her? Why is she never here?"

"Your sister," he breathed.

"Yes. She left our kingdom for yours, and we miss her."

"What kingdom is that? I have sought her in every kingdom I could reach, near and far."

"Ah, but hers is the kingdom of the sea." The daring sister swished her tail with a huge *thwack*, spraying salt water over the prince's velvet and silk. "Stay back," she commanded. "We have called her again and again. Always before, she came to our call. But now for three months she has not come. She would never leave you, not even to visit our grandmother. But she always came and sat with us here."

"Why did she never speak? You can."

"The sea witch got her tongue. She uses it too, or so I'm told. That was the price our sister paid to change her beautiful tail into those ugly legs, she who sang more sweetly than any of us. I love a handsome merman with black hair and yellow eyes. But she loved you. Grandmother says it's her fault, and she'll regret it for the rest of her three hundred years. But my sisters and I know you are in love with her. How could you not be? You'll marry her and share your soul, and everything will be all right. You do love her, don't you?"

He groaned. "I love her."

At that moment they both heard his wife's shrill voice. "Who's that hussy you're talking to? You, who won't talk to your own wife?" He looked up with a shudder, just in time to glimpse a flick of the mermaid's tail as she vanished again into the sea.

But now his wife's presence served only to remind the prince that he had lost the one who truly loved him. He could not bear to have the princess living in the same palace, however large it might be. He had her clothes and her jewels packed and sent her back to her parents with an armed escort for protection. So she too passes out of the story.

He summoned the most renowned sculptor in the kingdom, a tall woman with sinuous arms. "Make me a statue of my dear friend," he commanded, then entreated, "Let it be exact. Bring her alive before my eyes."

How could he know that the little mermaid had once made a garden under the sea and planted it with sea flowers red as the shining sun? In its center she had placed the statue of white marble that looked so much like him.

The prince created his own garden by the sea steps and planted it with lily of the valley, the leaves as green as sea lettuce and the clustered flowers like pearls. The sculptor chose a rosy marble for the statue. Perhaps on a whim, she gave the young woman a mermaid's tail. In the warm glow of the rising or setting sun, a watcher might easily imagine the stone to be alive. Now the prince's days were filled with dreams of his former companion's merkingdom far below the waves. He longed to visit her home, even though he knew he could not survive under the sea. He could not even seek the sea witch for a spell.

The sea called to him, and the five mermaid sisters came and sang to him and held out their arms. "He caused our sister's death," they told each other. "He married somebody else and our sister died."

"Come, human brother," they called to him. "Come home with us."

The next stormy night the waves came for him again and this time he did not hold the rail. He jumped into the water and caught hands with two of the mermaid sisters, diving with them to seek the sea kingdom from which his lost love had risen.

In her lair below, the sea witch cackled. From her false lips the prince heard at last the glorious voice of his dear one, singing to him of her love. Myriad creatures of the sea bottom stirred and reached upward with their tentacles. Skulls and skeletons, released from their grasp, floated free of their deadly embrace.

The sisters shuddered and tightened their grip on

the prince's hands. But he broke free and swam with desperate power toward the beloved voice, and toward the close embrace of the million tentacled creatures of the sea witch's domain. A forest of arms reached out and drew him in.

THE GOOD MOTHER

The giant clams were the real danger, but most of them would close up and bury themselves in the sand when the tide was out. It was possible to walk across to Grandma's island then, though later and earlier the cold salt ocean rushed and swirled among the rocks. The sound of the ocean was always in Ruby's ears. Sometimes it crashed, sometimes it growled, sometimes it murmured, but it was always there, defining and shaping her world. Years later, when she lived far inland, Ruby would lie sleepless night after night, missing that sound. She could never think about Grandma without her ears tingling and her nostrils prickling.

Ruby and her mum could easily walk to Grandma's house in twenty minutes. Ruby's mother carried her rifle in case of beasts, but neither of them had ever encountered one. The nearest major infestation was several hundred miles away. Woman and child did not bother to hush the sound of their footsteps on the path. Mum knew the tides. They always clambered over the driftwood on the beach just when the salt water had gone out enough for them to walk across the channel, stepping very carefully.

One day one clam was open a little, hiding under a huge mat of green-brown seaweed. It snapped shut on the edge of Ruby's cape. Luckily Mum had scissors in her bag. Both of them together couldn't pull the crimson velvet loose. Afterward Mum had to take a little tuck in the hem, but it didn't show. Months later Ruby was still having nightmares. "I wish Grandma had moved in with us years ago," said Mum one night after Ruby had wakened screaming. "It would make things so much easier now."

"Would Grandma leave her island?" Ruby was so startled she forgot her dream, in which a giant clam had closed on her leg above the knee. Grandma belonged in her rocking chair in the living room of the little brown house, or nestled in the quilts of her big carved bed.

"Don't look so shocked, child." Mum laughed wryly. "Sometimes people do move, you know. Things do change. But Grandma refused. 'I wouldn't be happy,' she told me, 'and nor would you.' Maybe she was right, who knows? It's too late now."

"Why?" asked Ruby. "Because of her heart?"

"That's right," Mum agreed. "Years ago, I might have persuaded her. Now I can't even try, she gets upset if she thinks I'm hinting. She's got her oxygen, and that's a blessing, she'd have died without it. I'm glad we didn't tell her about the clam nearly catching you. She'd worry, and there's nothing we can do."

Ruby never wore her precious cape again when she and Mum went out to the island. She wore tight leggings and a short jacket, and she and Mum watched out for clams. They both carried a stick to poke at any of the mammoth bivalves that got in their way. The two great shells would slam closed at a touch, and then they could get around the clam easily. The creatures took a long time to open again.

They couldn't go every day, only when Mum was off duty. Even then, if there was a beast attack anywhere she could not leave. Mum's job was to relay radio messages. Often she would be passing on a frantic call for help and relaying back a message of hope. The radio would crackle as routes were described to the hunters and schedules worked out. Mum's work saved lives.

There was a beast attack the day Grandma spilled her medicine. Mum's face grew rigid as her mother's apologetic voice came through. She ripped off her headset and jumped up. Then she sat down again. "What's to be done?" she fretted. "I won't be off duty until the hunters are on the way. It could be hours. I'll miss this tide and maybe the next one too. If Grandma doesn't get more medicine, she'll die."

"I can go to Grandma's by myself. Mum, you have to let me." Ruby's round face, lifted to her mother's, was red with frustration. "I'm ten years old. I'm not a baby. I can run faster than you can. I can be careful. I can swim if I have to."

"You know you can't swim there." Mum's hand trembled on Ruby's shoulder. "That current is so fast, it'd pull you off your feet and right into a clam. I don't want to let you go by yourself. What if a beast comes whispering along? What if a clam gets you? Oh, Ruby, what can I do?"

"I'll be okay. Don't worry, Mum, nothing's going to happen." Ruby patted her mother's hand.

Her mother shivered. "Take the basket, Ruby, and get along with you. Don't stop, but don't run, just keep moving and you should get there right on low tide. Wear your rubber boots, it'll be wet walking across." And there's a chance you could pull your foot out of the boot if a clam grabs at you, Mum thought. "Ruby, don't forget your stick."

"Mum, I'm scared about Grandma."

"I'm scared myself, Ruby, but you should be in time. Grandma's got her oxygen. She didn't spill all her medicine. She had one dose left in the bottle, and she radioed us for help immediately. Thank goodness I've been keeping a refill on hand. I knew she'd need it someday.

"When you get there, she'll be ready for her next dose. You give it to her. You have good steady hands, you won't spill. She'll be just fine. You put on the kettle and make her a cup of tea. Be careful when you pour the hot water, Ruby."

Ruby could hear the worry in Mum's voice. "I'll be fine, Mum. I'll look after Grandma. And I won't come back tonight."

"That's right. It's much too dangerous. Clams look like rocks in the dark, and beasts might be out hunting. I'll come for you at low tide tomorrow if I can get off the radio. If I can't come myself, I'll call for help, likely get one of the hunters. It's bright sun today, that should keep you safe. The sun, and your stick."

The wicker basket bumped awkwardly against Ruby's left leg as she clumped along the path, kicking at the dry leaves, swishing her stick. The autumn sun shone warm in the brilliant, unclouded sky. What child could be scared or worried on such a glorious day? Ruby ran a hundred yards or so for sheer delight. Then she dawdled, catching her breath. Walking onward, she stooped to pick wildflowers for Grandma, white Queen Anne's lace, yellow daisies, and tangled purple vetch. The tough stems bent but would not break for Ruby's chubby hands. She pulled the plants out, roots and all, adding them helter-skelter to the medicine and the bag of muffins in the basket. There was no point in hurrying. She could not go across until the tide was out.

"What are you doing, child? Does your mother know you're out?"

The gruff voice came from a dark thicket on her right. Ruby jumped, then slit her eyes, trying to see who—or what—spoke. Could the beasts really talk? Nobody ever said so, except in Grandma's stories. Ruby wished her hands were empty. "It's all right," the voice continued. "I'm a hunter. I get ready for beasts. Tell me, where do you go?"

"I'm taking Grandma her medicine across to the island. It's not dangerous. There aren't any beasts around here." Grown-ups were always in charge, Ruby knew. A child had to do what they said, especially a hunter. It was her or his job to keep people safe. "Mum knows I'm going," Ruby continued. "Grandma can't breathe if she doesn't get her medicine."

"Good child," the voice almost purred.

Basket and stick dropped from Ruby's hands. Her legs felt like big erasers, soft and bendy. "You're one of them, aren't you," she whispered, not knowing why she was so sure. "You're not a hunter. You're a beast." She ran in panic into the woods, away from the purry beast voice. Then she stopped. Was it coming after her? She listened—as if her life depended on it, Mum might say. Her life did depend on it. Mum had told her often enough what happened to people who got caught.

Nothing. Nothing.

Would she be able to hear it?

"One good thing about the beasts being so big," Grandma had told her, "they make a lot of noise. When Great-grandma was your age, there were lots of little creatures. Some of them were pets, but most were wild. Lots of life around then, all kinds, before the Chem Wars, and none of it could talk. Only people could talk, back then. That's how it should be. You could kill a wild mouse with a little trap and a bit of cheese. The only sound you'd hear would be the crack when the trap went off. Dirty things. I'm not sorry the mice are gone."

Ruby stopped running. She shut her mouth tight and held her nose to silence her laboring chest.

There was no sound of pursuit. She let out her breath in a long sigh.

The basket! Would it still be lying in the path? Would Grandma's precious medicine be safe? Now Ruby realized she must hurry. She must get across to the island before the tide turned.

Where was the path? Had she lost her way? Ruby looked behind her. She could not see through the bushes, but she knew the path must be that way. She had pushed through bushes as she ran. Hurry, hurry, sang her pulse. No, stop and listen, urged her brain. Her blood roared in her ears. Surely the beast was there, watching the path and waiting! But then she glimpsed the basket.

Without even a second's pause Ruby darted onto the path. She grabbed the basket with both hands and turned in a circle, all in the same motion. Nothing. The danger had gone away. Now she ran. Her side hurt. Her feet slipped inside the loose rubber boots. She could feel her socks bunching. How much farther?

Crashing, growling, the ocean pounded before her. Her nostrils prickled with the dank smell of kelp. Then she was into coarse sand, feet and boots slipping, almost tripping amid the rocks. Her stick must still be where she had dropped it when she ran from the beast. The tide was turning. Eddies tugged at her boots. Little waves swirled. Ruby fell once, but did not lose her grip on the precious basket. Several clams were out and open a little, waiting. Ruby managed to get around them easily enough. Once she poked a flower at a monster that filled the gap between two big rocks. It snapped shut. Ruby shivered as she climbed over it.

Nearing the other side at last, she pushed the basket onto a dark shelf of rock and scrambled up, scraping both legs. Ouch! Barnacles! Holes opened in her tights; the white exposed skin turned bright red immediately as blood spurted from the razor-sharp cuts. It didn't hurt, not yet, though she knew it would hurt a lot later. Any other time, Ruby would have been crying for a bandage and a hug. Now she was merely thankful. The nightmare was almost over. Up the path through the trees she could already glimpse the cedar shakes of Grandma's cottage.

Ruby bent to pick up her basket. But what was that mark in the sand? She moved the basket aside. Could it be a pawprint? It was almost as big around as the basket! The afternoon sky had clouded over. Soon the air would begin to cool. The dangerous dark would arrive. Ruby shivered and ran across the beach and up the path to Grandma's door.

Meanwhile, at the cottage, Grandma kept going to the door and opening it, looking for Ruby. Any other time she would have kept her home locked and barred. But her daughter had radioed to tell her Ruby was coming with the medicine. "The child!" Grandma had been horrified. "What if a clam gets her?" she screamed. "Or a beast? I'd rather take my chances without my medicine. It's no favor to me if Ruby gets hurt."

"Too late now." Mum had sounded very tired. "Relax, Mum, can't you? She's on her way."

So Grandma threw open her door as soon as she heard the knock. "You're here, Ruby," she cried. "Thank goodness you're safe, child. Come in, come in."

But Ruby did not come in.

Grandma peered into the outdoors. Her eyes saw —but her mind refused. Not furry legs! No, no. Not a long beast snout! No. In a merciful faint, Grandma dropped to the floor.

The beast squeezed her monstrous body through the narrow door with some difficulty. Once inside she tried to stand upright and banged her head. On all fours, however, she had ample room. The beast stared thoughtfully down at Grandma's body. Should she take it now to her hungry cubs? Her children would want it alive. They would want flowing blood to lick, and she would want twitching flesh to tear and chew. But the other one would come soon. More flesh, more blood.

The smoothskins are so small, the great beast thought. It'll take the two of them to make a decent meal. Food was getting harder and harder to find. Dimly the beast remembered earlier times, when almost any flesh had sufficed except that of her own kind. These days, fur, feather, fin made common cause against the smoothskins. The great beast would take other meat for her babies only if she had no choice.

She pulled the limp body of her catch along the floor and dumped it on the far side, between the low bed and the wall, where she could swat it down easily if need arose. The other smoothskin could run fast. How could she get it to come close enough to grab?

With her great paw she swatted at the big overhead light, only to leap back with a scream as pain jolted through her body. Trembling and weak, she climbed onto the bed and pulled the coverings over her hairy, furry self. If she lay sideways and bent her four strong legs, she could fit, though only just. The glare of light was gone; now she could see.

At once the creature saw the face beside the bed! She threw herself at it, landing in a tangle of claws and covers, the face crumpled under her. On the other side of the face was a long tube. The beast held the face tentatively to her own snout. She pulled the string attached to the face. The string jumped back against the face and hurt her other paw. Yes, she could put the face over her snout and pull the stretchy string over her head. The long tube went to a silver cylinder beside the bed. It smelled all wrong. It hurt to breathe. She tore off the face. Just the same, she would use the face when the little smoothskin came. It was the right size and shape for a smoothskin. It was not the right shape for a beast—too long and not enough snout—and what snout there was, was in the wrong place. But it would help trick the little smoothskin. Yes, it would certainly do that.

"Mother. Come in, Mother. Has Ruby got there yet? Come in."

The creature, still tangled in quilts and face, whirled around again.

The voice was coming from a box on top of a

table. The creature whipped the chair aside with one paw and nuzzled the box. What could this be?

"Mother. Are you all right, Mother? Come in. Come in."

Was this smoothskin inside the box? With one swipe the creature sent it flying. It crashed noisily to the floor. Buttons and knobs flew; sharp, gleaming shards fell out. The creature very cautiously picked up one long, bright sliver. Now she held the sliver against her own hairy epidermis. Ouch! Bright blood! She dropped the sliver and licked at her blood automatically. Then she bent and picked the gleaming, sharp thing up again. She might take it to her den. With it she could open the smoothskins' blood right over her babies' open mouths.

Rat-a-tat! Such a light tapping on the door! "Grandma! I'm here!" Such a little voice! A strange warmth tugged at the huge creature inside the cottage, akin somehow to the fierce love she felt for her own little ones. Her confused feelings, however, did not slow her responses. In one leap she gained the bed and fell on it, gathering the quilts about her as best she could. She reached for the face, ready to slip the stretchy cord around her head.

"Come in, dear," she called. Her voice sounded quivery to her own ears, echoing her shakiness. "It's not locked."

The door flew open and banged shut. Ruby threw the bolt before rushing over to the bed. "Here's your medicine, Grandma," she panted. "I ran as fast as I could. Oh, Grandma,"—the light voice quivered—"you needed your oxygen mask. I was too slow." The creature was totally still under the face and the quilts. "I'll just turn on the light," Ruby went on. "Then I can see to measure out your medicine. Ouch! This kettle is boiling. I guess you're ready for your tea."

Ruby's feet crunched on glass as she went to the light switch. Now that her eyes were getting used to the dim light, she could see the wreckage of the radio. Now she looked with new eyes at the bed, hearing again in her mind the purry voice from the woods. That mound on the bed was too big! Terror coursed through every vein. Ruby's mind blanked.

The covers moved a little. In horrid fascination Ruby watched. She glimpsed a vast paw, saw the dark triangle of a huge ear above the concealing mask. For a long moment, girl and beast were still.

Then the creature moved again. With a scream Ruby grabbed the big kettle and threw it, not noticing her own burned hands. Those hands threw back the bolt and opened the door in a single motion. Ruby ran uphill behind the cottage into the trees. No conscious thought was involved, but her feet headed away from the beach, where the current now boiled and surged. There would be no escape before the next low tide. Ruby was almost at the other end of the island before the pain in her side forced her to stop. She fell onto a mossy rock and sat, willing her laboring breath to quiet, listening for the beast.

Now she actually heard the sea sounds, the rhythmic crash of waves and the constant undertone of the immense ocean, the waters moving ceaselessly. As her ears adjusted, she began to distinguish the land sounds—cracks, rustles, birdcalls. Ruby cowered. As the minutes passed and nothing happened, the child's mind began to function again.

Grandma was dead. She must be dead.

What now? A cave? A tree? Anything was better than waiting for the creature to come. Then Ruby remembered her very own cave. She was sure it had once been a smugglers' cave, though she had found no gold or jewels; no liquor either, only three tall brown bottles against the back wall. "Beer bottles," Grandma had laughed. "Old ones, but lots of people used to drink beer like that. I did myself when I was young. We can pretend it was smugglers, can't we?"

Ruby's eyes stung. As she caught her breath, she was beginning to realize that she would never joke and laugh with Grandma again. Although she had not been to the cave for at least a year, she knew exactly where it was. In the fading light she clambered down over the boulders and around the prickly gorse to reach its entrance, not far above the surging waves.

What had changed? The entrance—it was bigger. Surely those two rocks had almost closed it off. Maybe not, it had been a long time. Ruby slipped inside. She always had to feel her way toward the shelf near the back. Long ago Grandma had given her a candle in a bright red candleholder and matches in a waterproof canister. "You can leave them in your cave," Grandma said. "These days, nobody else goes there. You can play smugglers and show a light for your pals."

Had her eyes adjusted more quickly, or was there

really more light? Hard to be sure. But the smell! Her cave had never smelled like this: sharp, pungent. Again Ruby stopped. Her eyes darted about the cave. What was that? Something . . . not very large. Her hands closed on the candle and matches. In the flickering light she sighed deeply; some of the tension began to pass.

Now Ruby could see what was making the smell. She knelt in wonder. Her free hand went gently toward one of the minuscule bodies. It stirred a little. A tiny mouth opened and made slurping, sucking noises. Then it closed again. The baby slept on. Ruby knew they were babies, but she had never seen babies like these. Four of them, and all four could have fitted easily into the basket she had carried to Grandma's house that very morning, so long ago.

"We had lots of pets when I was a child." Grandma could go on for hours talking about her terrier Samantha. "It was a big joke in our family. I named the dog Sam. What a surprise when Sam had puppies! My mother helped me find a better name. Ruby, Sam's two puppies were so tiny they could fit in my hand, both at the same time!" The big family album held several photos of little-girl Grandma wheeling the puppies in her doll carriage. The color had faded, but those little creatures looked very much like the four in front of Ruby now in the cave.

Ruby could hardly breathe. "I've wanted a pet forever," she whispered. "Please, little doggies, let one of you be mine."

On cue, one of the babies opened its sleepy eyes. Ruby put down her candle. Then she slid a hand under the tiny body and held its warmth, stroking and murmuring. This was better than her velvet cape! Again she remembered Grandma's words: "You'll never have a puppy, darling. All the dogs have died."

Could Grandma have been wrong? Whose babies could these be?

As she asked herself, Ruby knew. No wonder the cave entrance seemed bigger. She had run from Grandma's house right to the home of the beast!

Ruby ran from the cave without stopping to put down the baby or blow out the candle. At this end of the island there was no beach. The child looked over a small, rocky cliff to breakers that crashed against the rocks below. The day was darkening.

"I have to throw this little beast over the cliff into the waves," Ruby told herself. "I have to. Then I have to go back and get the others and throw them over too. I have to. They'll grow up and kill people. Their mother killed Grandma."

She hugged the warm little body tighter. The creature gave a startled yelp. "It's okay," sang Ruby, stroking it again. The little mouth found her finger. Noisily the baby began to suck. "You're hungry," said Ruby. "I haven't got any food. Poor little thing." She turned her back on the cliff and the waves and walked again toward Grandma's house. Perhaps she could put down the baby for the beast to pick up. Perhaps the beast would forget about her and look after its young.

By this time the beast was indeed intent on returning to her cubs with her one smoothskin. The kettleful of boiling water had burned her in spite of her fur, and she was still feeling shaky from the electric shock.

Grandma, on the other hand, was regaining her energy. Earlier she had started to come round and had managed to get the oxygen mask over her face without being noticed. Now, on her knees on the far side of the bed, she saw Ruby's basket lying in the broken glass on the floor. "Ruby, where are you?" she cried.

"The little smoothskin? She ran away," replied the beast. "I'll get her later. My babies and I need both of you."

"The stories are true, then. You can talk. I never believed it, not really."

"Believe whatever you like," said the beast indifferently. "You'll be just as good one way as another."

"Good for what? What do you need us for?"

"Food, of course." The beast sounded impatient.

"I need my medicine." The beast watched casually while Grandma plodded over to the basket. As she bent for the life-giving liquid, she glanced under her bed, checking the position of her old rifle. It had not been cleaned for months (everybody knew there were no beasts hereabouts), but it was loaded.

"I feel sick." The old woman lumbered back to the bed and fell on it. Her right hand reached down and closed on the stock of the gun. She swung it up fast, cocked, and fired. By the time the gun went off, the beast was on her and had seized it. The two great hairy forelegs bent the gun as if it had been a stick of eraser and tossed the debris out the door. "This fire stick killed my sister. This fire stick killed my mother." A flash of claws swept over Grandma's face, almost touching, almost slashing, but not quite.

I've still got the little revolver, Grandma thought. The tiny ivory-handled weapon was in the desk. In her head Grandma fired at the beast's head, at its belly, at the thickset neck. It would scarcely matter. She was no great pistol shot. The tiny bullets were meant to threaten a burglar, a human invader of times gone by. Like as not she'd miss completely. Even if her aim was good, a bit of lead might hurt the great beast but would hardly slow it down. Grandma looked at the clock. Six hours still to pass before the hunters could get across.

Why was she so sure that anybody would come?

Logic confirmed her intuition. The radio lay smashed on the floor. Her daughter would call and call and get no response. That would be enough. Now Ruby's mother would be getting frantic. Soon she would summon help. The hunters would have some distance to travel, but they could not get across until slack tide. Grandma had to force a delay.

Easy. Let the exhaustion in. Grandma let her muscles go limp. Let the beast see that the loss of the rifle had finished her. She closed her eyes.

The mask was suddenly pushed onto her face, the oxygen hissing. Grandma's faded blue eyes opened to the soft brown eyes of the beast. Its breath warmed her face; its pungent smell mixed with the oxygen in her nose.

"We must go soon," said the beast. "We must feed my cubs."

Grandma visualized her blood flowing, little creatures sucking.

"I'm tired," she sighed. "Wait a little."

The beast crouched. "This is not a good place," she said. "There is no food, and it is difficult to come and go." How could she safely move her tiny cubs? She could carry only one at a time, in her mouth. She would have to go quickly on the next tide. Other fire sticks would come.

"We go now," she ordered. "You go first."

"I must open the window," said Grandma. The casement beside the front door flew open at her touch as the beast's paw pushed her outside. While the gigantic creature struggled through the door, Grandma reached through the window and swung back the top of the desk. One swift motion and the little pistol was in her hands. There was no time to aim; she pointed and fired even as the huge paw swatted her to the ground.

At the side of the cottage, Ruby screamed. Her hands tightened convulsively; the cub squealed. The beast stood on three legs, the left forepaw raised, held protectively to its body, eyes fixed on cub and child. Grandma sat up slowly, her left arm dangling at an odd angle. Almost casually she tried to put it where it belonged; then the pain hit. She leaned weakly against the cottage.

Keeping her distance, Ruby walked forward until she was even with the front of the cottage. Now they could all see each other. Without speaking, Ruby began to edge her way backward down the slope that led to the sea.

"Stop," cried the beast. "Bring my baby." Her eyes darted to Grandma, then back to her child.

"No!" screamed Ruby. She turned and ran for the rocky, barnacled shelf she had climbed before. Below, the water swirled and rushed; waves crashed with their uneven repeated rhythm. Ruby held the baby away from her body. She turned sideways, watching but poised to whirl and throw the tiny beast.

The scene was frozen: Ruby with arms outstretched at the ocean's edge, the three-legged beast above her on the path, Grandma like a broken doll against the cottage. The beast baby squealed and wailed.

"Bring to me," entreated the beast. "See, I have blood." She lowered her paw. Ruby could see blood against the dark, hairy coat.

"Grandma," cried Ruby. "It's so little, Grandma. What should I do?"

"Make her move for it," called Grandma. "Put it down where you are, Ruby, and come up to me. Keep away from both of them."

Ruby had to force her body to obey. She had to make her back bend down, force her arms to lower the little creature to the soft moss, will her fingers to open and let go. Then she could move to Grandma, while the beast lumbered to her cub.

Time passed. Beast lay quiescent; cub drank and cuddled. Ruby tried and failed to pull Grandma's dislocated shoulder back into place. She carried blankets, painkillers, medicine, oxygen to her grandmother, then sat beside her. Time passed.

The beast was the first to rouse. "My other babies," she muttered. "I need them. They need food. I have food, but I cannot get to them. Too weak."

Ruby thought about the other little creatures. Tears gathered in her eyes. "Oh, Grandma, what should I do?"

Grandma considered. "Go and get them," she said at last. "Take the basket to put them in. I'll think about what to do when you get back."

But when Ruby got back with the basket full of wailing, naked little creatures, she could only run and hand them to their mother. "Grandma, they're so hungry," she gasped, and Grandma nodded as she ran by.

Blood still oozed from the tiny bullet hole above the beast's left paw, but very slowly. "Squeeze me," ordered the beast, "make blood come." Ruby's lungs were filled with the smell of beast as she massaged the hairy hide around the hole with both hands, urging out the blood, while in turn the mother held her little ones to drink.

The fourth cub opened sleepy eyes on Ruby, who picked it up and cuddled it again. Leaving the beast with the other three, she went back to Grandma. "It's a problem of food, as I see it," Grandma said slowly. "They can reason; they can talk; they have feelings. Food. That's the problem."

"Yes, Grandma," Ruby agreed.

"Babies used to have milk," said Grandma. "Milk from their mothers, or milk from cows, or milk from soybeans, it didn't matter. She hasn't got any milk for them, that's for sure. There haven't been any cows since I was your age, Ruby. But I've got soybean milk. Think I've even got a baby bottle. Climb up to the cupboard above the fridge, Ruby; use the stepstool. The bottle should be there. Soy milk's in the fridge. Fill the bottle and heat it for twenty seconds in the microwave. Can you do all that?" Grandma's voice was tender. Ruby returned her smile as she pushed open the door.

In a moment she was back, hurrying to the beast and the three still-hungry babies. "Food," said Ruby, in response to the beast's raised paw. The paw lowered, and Ruby picked up a little wailing body. In a moment the baby was sucking noisily. Ruby laid baby and bottle along the mother's vast forearm.

"Help me, Ruby," called Grandma. "I want to get down the slope there with the rest of you." Both faces were white and sweaty by the time Grandma was settled again.

"Here, take them." The beast handed another baby and the half-full bottle to Ruby. "Show me where it goes." She pointed to Grandma's dangling arm. Grandma nodded. Amazing that the huge paws could be so delicate! The paw on the beast's injured side braced Grandma while the other paw pulled and twisted. The shoulder was in again. Grandma's head lolled back against the beast. "Get the face for her," ordered the beast.

Ruby ran for the oxygen. For a while everything was in a muddle. Then Grandma was breathing well again and starting to get back some color. Ruby got another bottle of warm soy milk, and the last of the babies was fed. The beast's wound stopped bleeding.

They had hardly noticed how dark it had got. The tide would be on the ebb.

Grandma spoke at last. "You need food. We need protection against the clams. If you can tear them loose and bring them ashore, I can kill them. Is their flesh good food for you?"

"Likely," replied the beast. "If I am careful, I can tear a clam out of the sea and bring it onto land, but then it will not open, not until it has died and the flesh has died and it is not good anymore."

"Can you manage to come down closer to the shore?" asked Grandma. "Let's see what we can do."

"How kill them?"

"The old clambake barrel," said Grandma. "It held enough clams for a hundred people. Or the sap kettle. Haven't used either one of them in forty years! We'll build a fire under the barrel and fill it with water. Drop a clam in and it will open and die. The little ones did. Don't see why the big ones would be any different."

"All right," agreed the beast. "We will go to the shore."

In the moonlight the three stared down. The channel was almost bare again. They could all see one of the giant clams, open a little, waiting greedily. Grandma reached down with a long stick. The clamshells thudded closed. Lightly the beast bounded to the ocean floor. Out came the great talons; the right paw swung beneath the clam.

Bang!

The beast was hurled backward. Into the opening between creature and clam Ruby leapt. "Stop shooting, you hunters," cried Grandma. "I knew you'd be here, and I forgot. Stop shooting now. Careful, child, crouch down," she called to Ruby, who was standing as best she could in front of the great beast.

Another shot rang out. Ruby fell back. "Stop it!" Grandma was screaming now. The shooting stopped.

Ruby was not afraid. Grandma would make the hunters help her and the beast. The girl lay against the hairy creature, breathing its pungent smell. It wrapped a huge paw around her, holding her warmly, putting pressure on her slim white arm where blood was spurting. Above the steady pulse of the ocean, another steady beat filled the child's ears: the beast's own strongly beating heart. Ruby looked up. From this angle, the creature's eyes and ears weren't big at all.

Nor were its teeth.

A TASTE
FOR BEAUTY

*W*hump. *Snap.* "Help!"
  Whump. Snap. "Help!"
Over and over, those sounds still chase each other through my mind. Especially on Saturday nights, when I am accustomed to sit with a book in my lap in a corner of the library. I wish I could read the book. I listen perforce to the endless round in my head: *Whump. Snap.* "Help!"

The first two sounds are Pa hitting Mum and something breaking. The third one is her scream. It is always a thin scream, thready, lacking all sense of vitality or power. Just like Mum.

Pa was my stepfather, but the only father I ever knew. His regular Saturday-night entertainment included beating up Mum. Still does, for all I know. Any old Saturday night, you could depend on it. The bars would close, and Pa would come home and begin. I never could figure out why Mum stayed home. He went to hit me once and I grabbed a knife. He never tried that again. I loathe Pa with a passion.

I always knew I'd run away when I could. The first time, I was ten years old. The police brought me home. Home! That's a stupid word for it. They brought me back to our house. Mum locked me in my room for three days. I had bread and water to eat and one bucket to wash in and another one instead of a toilet. My room sure did stink. "I'll kill you if you do that again," I told Mum. I meant it too.

After that I got the abattoir job. To start with, I sharpened the knives and brought them to the assembly-line workers who cut the animals' throats and slit their bellies. Soon I graduated to the line myself. At first I thought I'd be upset, but I pretended I was killing Pa. No sweat. It wasn't more than a month before I was getting the biggest bonus for the fastest, cleanest work. A firm hand and total conviction, and you can't stop to think, except about being the best. The best. The quintessential best.

The men all had pinups on their lockers. *Playboy* girls with the names of different months. They liked to whistle at me and reach out a hand as I went by. "None of this shit," I warned them, and they did catch on very quickly after I slashed Tom's pants in a sensitive area. "I'm faster with my knife than any of the rest of you," I reminded them, "and don't you forget it."

George was the foreman. One day he brought me a huge bag of makeup and a poster about a beauty contest. "Don't get me wrong," he said carefully, "all I want you to do is look."

"Fifty thousand dollars to the most beautiful girl in the land," said the poster. "Royal judge," it said.

"I think you could win," George told me. "I've been watching you, kid. You got class, you got drive, you got looks. We've got a year to get ready. Give you a quarter of a chance, and you are going right to the top. And I, kiddo, I am going to be right on your tail."

I felt like an animal as George's eyes moved slowly up and down. "I'll bet on you to win," he continued. "Right on the nose! Of course, there's a whole lot you'll have to learn. I'll stake you to some modeling courses and all the other junk. If you win, I get half the money, after expenses." He leered at me. "I might even marry you."

"No way, fatso," I said. "But I'll make a deal with you for the training. Okay."

"That's dumb," said my mum when I quit the abattoir job. "You, a model!" She laughed.

Pa's fist clenched and the little blood vessels in his face stood out angry and red. My knife was on the hall table, along with my other stuff from the abattoir. I just looked at it and smiled until Pa looked at it as well. "I'm the fastest, Pa," I reminded him, "just in case you were thinking of starting anything. I'm faster with that knife than any fuckin' *man* at the plant. I'm just reminding you."

"You can leave here anytime," he said, "only you keep on paying room and board just the same."

I almost said "Make me," and then I bit my tongue. No sense pushing Pa any further right then. They'd have a hard time getting money from me after I was gone.

I never knew it took so much work to be beautiful. My day started with gym at six in the morning. Every day. Speech therapy at nine. Deportment, that slinking model's walk, at ten. Makeup and fashion from eleven till one-thirty, with a diet fruit plate for lunch. Dancing class at two. School from three to five, with homework every night. Dentist once a week until all my teeth had caps or were filed down even and white. Bed at nine—ten on Saturday night.

I'm no athlete, and I never trained for the Olympics, but this was the beauty Olympics I was training for, and I'm a winner. Lots of times I wanted to give up, just the same. Speech class was the hardest. After five years at the abattoir I did not have the cleanest mouth in town. But dance class was tough too. One day the dance director told me I was as graceful as a water buffalo in a rice paddy. I walked out and went back to the abattoir. "You get your butt back in class," yelled George. "I've got a stake in you."

I looked at him. I'd forgotten how cold the abattoir was. I'd forgotten the stink of it. I looked at Jenny's hands, red and cracked from water and blood, and remembered how ugly my hands used to be, and how they used to hurt. I looked at George and pretended he was a cockroach for a minute while I thought it over. Then I went back to my dancing class.

Sometimes I wondered how much of the fifty thousand would be left to divide, even if I won the contest. It wasn't just the classes. I had boxes and bags of makeup. I had three closets full of clothes, designer stuff, nothing ordinary. I counted my shoes once: seventy-two pairs.

What would have happened if I'd never met Esmeralda? I think about how different my whole life would have been, but then I tell myself I'm being silly. Esmeralda and I were meant to meet. I was starting to do little modeling shows by then, afternoon shows at local shopping malls. Esmeralda was reading teacups and telling the future in her crystal ball. I didn't believe in any of that stuff in those days, but the lady in charge of the models gave us all a present of a reading, just for fun.

The Incredible Esmeralda surged from her chair as I approached. Incredible was the right word. She towered a foot above me. Skirts billowed below and a vast bust jutted above a waist no larger than my own, cinched with a jeweled girdle.

"I've been waiting for you," Esmeralda told me. She had a puffy chipmunk face, square lips painted boldly red. The light glinted on her gold teeth as she spoke. I was certain I had never seen her before in my life.

Esmeralda sank into her chair, which vanished beneath her massive contours. Ignoring me, she became totally engrossed in the shimmering crystal of her ball. "Come over here beside me," she said at last. "Look deep."

"She's beautiful," I whispered, staring in at the slim queen standing there. She was tiny, and glorious in her jeweled coronet and scarlet gown. The dress looked like silk velvet, so soft, so real that I reached out a hand to stroke it and was amazed to find my hand stopped by the cold, hard glass.

Esmeralda cackled. "Look at her face," she said.

"It's me," I gasped.

It was me, it really was, dressed in those royal robes. My long hair was braided in and out around the glittering crown, shining black against the jeweled gold.

Oh, I thought, a modeling job where I'm dressed like a queen! But no, the scene changed and there she was—I was—in white ermine, sitting on a throne beside the king. I felt dizzy. I couldn't get my breath.

"Yes, it's you," said Esmeralda softly. "It's you. Learn from me and it will all come true."

"And what in return?" I asked.

The square lips curved in a cruel smile. "You must in return do one small thing for me. Or perhaps not so small. You shall know on the eve of the contest what it is to be."

If I were queen, I'd be safe forever. I could put Pa in jail if I wanted. I could have him hanged. I didn't know Esmeralda then and put little faith in her prophecy, or I might have hesitated about pledging I knew not what. Lightly I spoke the fatal words. "If I become queen, I'll do one thing for you, large or small," said I.

After that, I had my lessons with Esmeralda to work into my schedule. Potions. Spells. Enchantments. Telling the future. Looking into the past. She mostly collected the mugwort and vervain, the mouse's tails or the mustard seed, everything we needed. But I had to learn where to find it all and how to use it. "I won't always be around to help you," Esmeralda warned.

So much to learn!—and only a few weeks now until the big contest. The king was to be the royal judge, I knew that. I had to be ready by then to put him under my spell.

On the eve of the contest, Esmeralda came to claim my pledge. My face prickled as she spoke. I put both hands on the back of my chair to steady myself. "I don't understand," I told her. "I'm not fond of children, sniveling brats, but if I'm to kill for you, Esmeralda, I must know why."

"You kill for yourself as much as for me," she told me. "You kill to protect your own position, as you shall realize. But hold and attend, for I speak to you of solemn matters of great antiquity."

Esmeralda stood tall. Her great curved earrings dangled almost to her shoulders; the stones caught the light and flashed a deep blue as brilliant as her eyes, and full as cold. I had thought them mere gaudy trinkets, but realized suddenly and with awe as she continued speaking that they were sapphires and diamonds. No doubt the thick ropes of gold that hung almost to her waist were real as well.

"My grandmothers and great-grandmothers were queens," she said, "Romany queens. Gypsies. We ruled no country, but many people in many lands gave homage to us. In great matters we commanded absolute obedience, cheerfully given, for my fore-mothers were women of amazing wisdom.

"Three queens in three generations were cruelly murdered by kings in this land. Those kings were ancestors of the king here, just as those murdered queens were ancestors of mine. A few women of our line survived, a pitiful few. We swore a blood oath to avenge those three deaths on every female of this royal line. Let the kings live, as my great-grandfathers lived, in pain and loss.

"Be advised: never bear this king a child. For more than a century, no female born to his line has survived her tenth year of life. Few brides have lived into their second decade of marriage.

"We don't take them immediately. If a king is to suffer, he must grow to love his wife or daughter. But we have never failed."

I shuddered. "The king's first wife? Her death in childbirth? Was that your work?"

"I was the midwife." Esmeralda's hands sketched a parody of cruel death. "But the child's death will be no loss to you; gain rather, for she is a dangerous rival for the king's affection. For yourself, have no fear," she added quickly. "I guarantee your safety. You are ours in life, not death."

Her eyes held mine. My shudder passed.

My costumes for the competition were ready. The bathing suit was shimmering silver and black, and the strapless evening gown was gold, embroidered with rubies and emeralds on its billowing skirts. But black visions rose between me and the precious clothes. "I can't do it," I told Esmeralda.

"You can," she replied. "You must. The king is just another man, no different from your pa. Here,

104

look at this." She uncovered a plain oval mirror with a black frame. Ugly-looking thing.

"Speak to it," said Esmeralda. "Say, 'Mirror, mirror, on the wall, Who is most beautiful of all?'"

Talking to a mirror! I'm not crazy. But I'd seen many strange things by then in Esmeralda's company. I still felt very shaken, but I said it, and then there was a voice from the mirror. It said, "You are most beautiful of all."

A talking mirror! The oddest part was that I believed it. Everything felt as if it was meant to be, including my pledge to Esmeralda. I calmed right down. I breezed through that competition, smiling all the way. It was easy to slip the magic pill into the king's drink, easy to walk across the stage and preen and turn, easy to swing my heavy skirts.

It was no surprise when I won the beauty contest. It was no surprise when I married the widowed king. His daughter, pale little black-haired thing, was flower girl at our wedding. Snow. What a stupid name. Might as well have called her Rain, or Hail, or Sleet.

After my first searching look, I paid as little attention to her as possible. I carefully didn't think about the promise I had made to Esmeralda and sealed with a drop of my blood. It may be hard to believe, but I had really forgotten all about it when the mirror changed its message and told me my stepdaughter, Snow, was more beautiful than I. I never did like children, but I didn't want to think of killing her, even though I hated her father to spend time with her, time stolen from me.

But the mirror's new message changed everything.

I have to be the most beautiful, anybody can understand that. I have to have the king most in love with me. It doesn't matter what people say about character and intelligence being important and beauty being only skin deep. I know better. Nobody ever said much about my character and intelligence. I became queen because I'm most beautiful of all. I look at Snow White now and think about the abattoir. I think about Mum and Pa. I think about Esmeralda too. She wants me to keep my promise, either in person or by proxy. "I only want what's best for you," she says.

Esmeralda suggests I should talk to Gerald, my husband's chief huntsman. Gerald looks at me with lovesick, longing eyes. He says there is nothing he would not do for me. Perhaps this is true. Somehow I hesitate to put it to the test.

Happily, I don't need to put it to the test. I don't need Gerald. I have got out my book of poisons, but I'm really more comfortable with knives. I have sharpened my long steel knife and my little pointy one. I think all the time about Snow White lying dead. I can take care of her myself. It won't be difficult at all.

THE WOODCUTTER'S WIFE

The story that I intended to eat them is a fabrication. People will make up anything. I did intend to observe them closely under conditions of stress, and more blood would have been very useful to me.

In the end, I would probably have let them go back home. Their father, my husband, was making my life as wretched as his own. In the end, it would have been a choice between having the children back and pretending (for a while) to be a happy-ever-after fairy-tale family, or getting rid of all three of them and moving on.

Witchcraftly skill like mine has its drawbacks. When I take on human form, I age very little. In my true form, however, I am as old and hooknosed as they come, cheeks sunken, red eyes bleared and rheumy. I'm tired, and getting more tired day by day. After the three hundredth birthday, there's not a lot one can do. All my power goes into keeping myself alive in my real form and maintaining my

107

current transformation. Occasionally I find the energy to stir up a potion or weave a simple spell.

Does it seem strange that I have transformed to a poor woman, a woodcutter's wife? Wealth and power lose their charm when the novelty wears off. I've had my fill of both. In truth, a plain homespun dress and pattens take less energy than fancy silks covered with gold thread and pearls, and it's a smaller change from my real self to this middle-aged housewife than to a beautiful woman, be she old or young.

Besides, he was not poor when I married him: young, beautiful, and strong. Good too. They say opposites attract. His goodness appealed then, though that appeal quickly palled; the man has bored me to distraction these many years.

In an earlier transformation I went in for great beauty. I had a mirror to tell me so: a nice touch. Being beautiful is a full-time job, even with power such as mine was then. And do what one will, one gets older and loses it. My transformations must all age, however slowly. Eternal youth attracts much too much attention. I have nothing against age; experience accompanies it.

It was simpler being a woodcutter's wife than being a queen. My days were my own. When Karl went off to work in the forest with the children, I could adopt my real form and do some work of my own.

The most potent spells have always demanded human flesh or blood. Everyone knows about the Hand of Glory. It does indeed permit me to go at will into a house at night, certain that no sleeper shall awaken. But simply to cut off the hand of a hanged man is not enough. The hand is necessary, but not sufficient. It must be taken at a certain time and in a certain way and the spell cast truly. My Hand belonged to my husband the highwayman. We were together for ten happily eventful years a century ago. Then he cast his eyes toward a young gypsy woman. I did not wait for his unfaithfulness; next night the redcoats lay in wait for him. I have no energy to go far these years, but occasionally I would take his Hand from its hiding place and watch the slumber of Karl and the two children. Under its power they never stirred, but sometimes terror filled a face, or lips formed a soundless scream. When my need was great, I could draw off a cup of their blood, though not often. The children became pallid, and Karl could not work as vigorously as usual. No doubt this is partly why we became so desperately poor.

I watched our food dwindle almost to nothing, and did not act quickly enough. Without flesh to eat, I lacked the energy to transform. In my own shape, even though my eyes are dim, my nose is sharp. Odors float to me; then I can point at an animal and it comes to my oven. But at that time I was dependent on a loaf of bread and a jug of milk.

I remember snapping at the child, "Gretel, bring me that milk. Quickly, now!"

"Right away, Stepmother."

"Gretel, watch that broom!"

Too late. "Stupid child! Our last milk—and our

last jug. A spoon, and here's a dish. Try and save some. Idiot child, I'll whip you till you bleed for this."

Hansel's voice behind me. "You're not our mother. You can't whip us. Only Dad."

I feel it all again. Rage flares in me, the power of anger. I must get away while this strength lasts. I must transform. They are not going to defy me and get away with it. Of course they don't follow me into the forest. Around the first bend in the path, I take my rightful form. Surely this rage will propel me safely to my little forest hut, where there is flesh to restore my strength. Come, my broom, it is not far to go.

Gretel did me a favor when she made me so angry. I must not forget again the power of rage. This stew has waited for me for six months. Under my spell it remained fresh and hot. How good it is. I feel the blood in my veins. Energy! Power! I could have died in that stupid woman's body. I won't risk that again. But what to do?

Yes, the plan was forming. I could see it all. A few preparations and I'd be ready to go back.

"There's only bread for supper, Karl, and water to wash it down."

"I broke the jug, Daddy, and all the milk got spilled. I'm sorry, I'm sorry."

"Don't cry so hard, Gretel, love. I'll think of something. I love you. It was an accident, I know. Here, have some of my bread."

When I wasn't bored with Karl's goodness, I'd be furious. "She spilled the last drop of milk. We all have to go hungry. I said she couldn't have any bread."

"She's just a baby," Karl replied, holding out his whole piece. Gretel broke it carefully in half—she's a very precise child—and handed half back. They munched quite contentedly, as if we had a house full of food, and money to buy more.

I held back my rage and contemplated my plan. Admirable! After the children had gone to bed, Karl sat wearily staring into the fire. "I don't know what to do," he said. "Helga, what on earth are we going to do? I cut so little wood these days, and it's so far to town to sell it. If I had a horse to pull the cart, it would be easy—but if we had had a horse, we would have had to sell it or eat it long since. I don't know where to get food for the children."

That Karl! He didn't say anything about food for us! I made my face all soft and tender. "It's dreadful, Karl, dreadful. We can't sit by and see them starve to death. Us too, but we'll last longer than the children."

"I know. I can't bear it."

"I don't have any easy suggestion, Karl, and I can't solve it. We're all going to die. We have to accept that. The only thing I can think of is to make it quicker and easier for the little ones."

"Kill them?" His face was full of horror.

"No, no, of course not. We'll take them into the forest. We can build a big fire for them and leave them while we work, just like you always do. I'll go with you, Karl. If we take them far enough, they won't find their way back, and the end will be quick.

I know it's horrible, dear husband, but I'm like you, I can't bear to watch them die."

I just looked at him, waiting for his will to crumble. I have eaten; he has not. My will is centuries strong.

"Tomorrow," he mumbled at last.

I slept well, but his side of the bed was tumbled and tossed; his face was gray as we got up and had our breakfast of water and a mouthful or two of bread.

"We're all going to the forest today," I said brightly. "Won't that be nice?"

Hansel looked at me. His eyes are very dark, almost black. Karl usually cuts his hair, but he has not done so lately, and dark curls frame Hansel's thin face. It was a considering look, almost judgmental it felt, but Hansel spoke evenly enough. "Yes, Stepmother," he said.

Karl and I led the party. Gretel was sobbing bitterly, almost as if she knew! But of course she couldn't know. "Come along, child," I said, in my best bracing-but-kind tone. "Hansel, why are you looking back?"

"I'm looking at a little bird sitting on the chimney," said Hansel. "It's almost as if it is trying to speak to me."

"Come along," I said, "move your legs." Karl said nothing. He has no talent for conversation.

The common story is right about what happened next. Hansel had indeed managed to overhear me talking to his father. While I slept, the brat had gone out and filled both pockets with white stones. We built the fire and left them, but they were back with the dawn the next day.

"Thank God," said Karl. "Thank God." He could say nothing else, but he hugged the thin bodies and his face shone through his tears.

"We'll come with you to town, Father," said Hansel. "I can help you pull the cart. Gretel can walk very well. She won't hold us up."

They came back in the evening laughing and crying by turns as they told me the story. In the market, a rich merchant had taken one look at Gretel and bought all the wood. He had his own servants pull the cart home while he took father and children to the tavern for a hot meal. Then he filled the cart with food: sacks of flour, meal, potatoes, a pail of honey, a box packed with meat, butter and eggs, jugs of milk and wine. Atop the load he set a crate with six laying hens, who squawked and chattered when I set it down as if already they felt my eyes piercing their hearts.

"It's wonderful," I lied, cursing the man who had interfered with my plans, "but why on earth did a total stranger do all that?"

Karl's face grew solemn. "He told me his little daughter died not long ago. Gretel reminded him of her. He said she reminded him too much of how she looked before she died; he wanted Gretel to be healthy and well. 'Give her an egg every day,' he told us." Karl shook his head.

"It's a wonder he didn't want to keep her," I remarked.

"He did." Karl's voice was taut. "Yesterday I

might have had a different answer. Food in your belly does make things look different, that's a fact. Today I told him nothing on earth would make me part with my darling. 'That's right,' said the merchant, 'that's just how I felt.' There were tears in his eyes. 'I would never come in the way of a father's love,' the man told me." Karl's arms tightened around Gretel; then he reached out to hug Hansel as well. "The merchant knew you needed food too," he said. "He thought you were a fine boy."

"So all's well that ends well," said I lightly, putting the big stewpot on the hob. "What a dinner we'll have!"

Next thing you know, they were dancing and singing in a circle, Karl bending to take the children's hands. Faster and faster they spun; I got tired and dizzy just looking. "Enough," I said, trying not to sound cross. "Gretel, you set the table. Hansel, bring more wood and then sweep the floor. Karl, you get Grandma's table cover out of the chest. Let's get ready for our feast."

The merchant's gift brought us luck. Nor did his kindness stop there. He sent a servant out to our hut the following day, leading a cow. "Milk for the little ones" was the message. The servant said his master did not want to see Gretel again, but he wanted all of us to be well and happy for her sake.

A witch learns patience in three hundred years. Hansel and Gretel fed the fowl and gathered the eggs. I milked the cow and churned the butter. Karl chopped wood and hauled it to town to sell. "I'll be able to get a horse and cart again, if this keeps up," he said, smiling. I kept up my energy and bided my time. When the children went with their father, it was easy to transform. I did not take any blood, except now and then a cup or so from the cow. Karl was cutting a lot more wood. "I've got my heart in it," said he, but I knew that good food and no blood loss were the reasons.

"A good heart," I told him, and so indeed he had. Bovine, banal, and good.

I bided my time.

First the cow dried up. "She needs freshening," said Karl. But we did not know anyone with a bull. So there was no more milk or butter. The hens gradually stopped laying. We had no rooster, so could never hatch any young. One by one the hens were stewed for dinner. The children wept. They had named the hens. The day we ate Patience, the last of them, I knew we were on the road to starvation again.

This time my plans were thorough. Food for me was hidden in the root cellar, under the sand. No chance this time that I would lack energy to transform. The stew was kept hot and fresh by one of my simpler spells, which also prevented any odor from leaking up to hungry noses.

Karl sold the cow. I told him he should go back to the merchant for more help, but he refused. "I'm no beggar, and you know it," he told me roughly. Yes, I knew, but I also knew he would have been thinking of it. After his words to me, he'd put it off awhile, even though Gretel was pale and thin. I needed time to go to town and arrange an accident. By the time

Karl finally went to the merchant's house, the man had lain a month in his grave.

The price of the cow kept us through that winter, and Karl's woodcutting kept us through the following summer and fall. Then it was winter again, and again there came a day when we were down to our last jug of milk, our last loaf. Gretel did not drop the jug this time; with that one change, history repeated itself.

But this time I locked the door.

It was harder and at the same time easier to persuade Karl to abandon the children again in the forest. I wouldn't have thought any parent could become more besotted with a child than Karl had been already with Gretel, or prouder of a child than he had been of Hansel. He had taken to calling the day they returned the miracle day. "There were two miracles," he said. "The children found their way home. That's number one. And then all that wonderful food! Two miracles on the same day. Surely we are blessed, Helga," he would say. But not recently. He watched as the children again became pallid and gaunt, stared wordlessly as their laughter faded into silence.

"Yes," he said finally. "I cannot bear to see them suffer, Helga. It's worse than last time. I was so sure we were saved forever. This time it is harder. We will take them into the forest again. And this time we will take them deeper, as you say." He groaned. If I had been capable of pity, I might have pitied him then.

"Maybe there will be another miracle," I suggested.

Hope leapt in his eyes. "My very thought," he breathed. "Maybe a better miracle. Maybe."

As we set out the next morning, I paid more attention to Hansel than I had last time. Again he and Gretel lagged behind. Again Karl and I saw them turn to look back at the house. "What are you looking at now?" I asked at last. "It's getting late. It's hard enough to get a good load of wood without you holding us back."

"I'm just looking at the roof," Hansel replied. "Do you remember where my white cat used to sit, right beside the chimney? I'm thinking of her."

"Do you still miss her?" asked Karl. "Cats do just disappear sometimes, but it was very sad."

"Just as well," I said, remembering how that cat had fought as I twisted its neck, remembering the love potion I had made with its heart's blood. "Just as well, we couldn't have fed it anyway." We made our way onward in silence.

Again we lit a fire to keep the children warm. I set a little spell on a maple branch so that it would keep hitting an adjoining branch. To the children it would sound like an ax. They would be sure their father was not far away. Again we worked for part of the day, gradually making our way home.

Now that the children were gone, I could transform as soon as Karl had entered the forest. Every day I quickly flew the short distance by air to my hidden hut. I could see the children in the forest and could make an excellent guess as to when they would come across it as they wandered. They had never seen me in any form other than that of their stepmother. Even as a witch, I can put on a pleasant smile and warm manner when need arises.

The difficult part of my preparation was transforming the hut. None of the stories has ever done justice to my creativity. The windowpanes were of spun sugar, the story says. It does not add that they were a perfect one-way mirror. I could see out, but nobody could see in. The roof was gingerbread. It was a kind of gingerbread cake, with whipped cream on top. I didn't think the children would notice or care that there was no snow on the ground. The walls were sturdy gingerbread, with jujubes, jelly beans, and peppermint patties held on with icing. The doorsill and the door itself were blocks of chocolate. Inside, the cottage looked charming. It was charming—and charmed. I dreamed up the whole thing. Nobody ever built a gingerbread house before me.

It was a gigantic task, almost beyond my waning powers. All the spells I had stored over the years went to help build that sweet house. The result, no doubt of it at all, would be irresistible to a child.

I could hear them coming a long way off. I managed to waft the peppermint, chocolate, butterscotch, raspberry cheesecake smell of the place toward them. It worked! Minutes later, my little victims approached. Ha! I listened to them crunch and gnaw. At first they swallowed before they chewed.

Later their manners became more civilized. When I thought they'd had enough to make them sick, I went out to give 'em hell for stealing my house.

"Sorry," said Gretel. Hansel remained silent. "We were starving," pleaded Gretel.

"That's no excuse," I began to say, and then realized I was saying exactly what their stepmother would say in such an event. I stopped in midbreath. My voice and form were so different that they'd never recognize me, but mannerisms, tone of voice might still betray.

"Come in," I invited. "I was just going to make tea."

"We can't stay, thank you," said Hansel politely. "We're not allowed."

"Thank you," said Gretel, with tears in her pretty blue eyes, "it's very kind of you." She followed me inside my chocolate door, and Hansel, scuffling his feet, followed unwillingly. "How beautiful," breathed Gretel, looking greedily around. Inside, the place was full of bright silks and brocades. I gave them delicate teas from cups of translucent china, along with food such as they had dreamed of but never eaten. Their eyes were closing as they ate, hunger and exhaustion warring in each scrawny body.

"This is better than the forest, isn't it?" I inquired as I led them to the bedroom. Four tired eyes rested longingly on two down-covered beds. Less than a minute later by the clock, both were dead to the world. I wouldn't need my Hand of Glory if I wanted their blood. However, neither child had any blood to spare. I knew they would serve my purposes much better when they were rested and fed.

By morning my preparations for my young guests were complete. I asked Hansel to go into the stable to feed my horse. Then I clasped the padlock shut on the closed door. I did laugh when he tried to get out, though stories lie that say I cackled in glee. And certainly I did not bother to keep up the magic of the silk comforters. Let Gretel sleep with rags of blanket to keep her warm!

I really needed a servant to do all my work. My 313th birthday was coming up. I had every right to feel tired. Gretel was admirable. The smallest threat to Hansel sufficed. "That floor is still dirty. Scrub it again, or Hansel goes hungry tonight!" And the floor would be scrubbed until it sparkled. Actually I wanted to fatten them both. I didn't want Hansel to miss any meals, but there was no real danger that I'd have to carry out my threats. Gretel was taking no chances at all.

The stories make me out an awful fool. "Hansel, stick your finger through the bars," they say I'd say, and Hansel would stick out a little bone. "Too thin to eat yet," they say I'd say, smiling a little with my withered mouth.

I don't like to look at my real face in the mirror. Most of my teeth are gone, and it takes energy to keep even a few false teeth in place with magic spells. That's why I eat stew these days: the meat is very soft. I have eaten human flesh, but not for more than a hundred years. Hansel was still young and tender, though not as tender as Gretel would be. But they could be killed and eaten only once. It would have been a very great waste. Alive and fat, they could supply blood for all the spells I would ever need.

Of course I knew Hansel was not sticking his finger out for me to feel. My eyesight is getting worse and worse, but my nose has not betrayed me, nor have my hands. My fingers know the difference between skin and bone.

All this time, I transformed at night and went home to be a loving wife to Karl. It added variety to my life to feed his guilt about the children, to put into his head subtle suggestions about animals, to nourish his nightmares. He stopped cutting wood and took to roaming the forest all day, looking and calling, returning exhausted at night, only to be exhausted even more by his horrid dreams. At what point would he be actually, irretrievably mad? I fed him twice a day, good meals, and he never even asked where the food was coming from, just ate weeping and slept with nightmares and went crying about the forest, never coming close to my little house; I made sure of that!

I had little philosophical conversations with Hansel. "What would happen if I ate you a little bit at a time? I could cut off one of your arms and begin on that. I am a witch, you know, Hansel, I could heal the stump and it wouldn't even bleed. Which arm would you like me to take first?"

Gretel only screamed and threw herself on the floor if I talked like that, and she was useless as a servant for several hours afterward, but Hansel would consider the topic gravely and reply evenly, as if it concerned him not at all, "I am sure I would not be good to eat. But you wouldn't need to take a whole arm to find that out. A piece of flesh would serve that purpose and leave me all my arms and legs. You might want me to do some heavy work for you sometime. I think you would want to make sure I am still able."

"We'll see," I'd say, and stomp off angrily. Of course I wanted him able to do the heavy work when needed. I wanted to enlarge my lab before winter, and it would be much easier on me for Hansel to construct it. My power continues, alas, to wane.

So that bit about the oven, and Gretel tricking me into it, that part is so much malarkey, as my Irish husband used to say. There was an oven, and I did have bread to bake, and I was teasing Gretel about baking Hansel in that oven, but I never told her to get into it to test it. That would be absurd. I had taken too much for granted, however. Gretel was not as submissive as she seemed. Wretched child!

How could she have managed to find the key to Hansel's padlock? The spell of invisibility ought to have lasted forever. Still, the day came when Hansel was not inside the stable but around the side of it, and the two of them did manage to push me inside and close the lock. Again a purple rage seized me. However, I was too well nourished to use its power well. I seized the bars. A hundred years ago they would have given way like kindling. Now, however, they resisted me. I fell to the ground, overcome for the moment by my anger.

That must have been when the children pried open my jewel chest and filled their pockets. Likely they also took a satchel full of gems. My great topaz amulet was gone, along with the maharajah's emerald crown and the diamond of Zanzibar. I did not make a tally until much later, however. When I came to my senses, the children had fled and I was still imprisoned. If I transformed, I would lose my power. Should I change my transformation? A bird or insect or small animal could easily pass between the bars. However, I have energy to do this only once. Whatever transformation I take now, I'll have to keep for a long time, perhaps forever. What shall I do?

Could a skinny, scrawny child slip between these bars? How small would I have to be? Am I ready?

And if I do it, what then? Karl will have lost his wife. But the children will find him. They will have lots of food, and he roams the forest every day. They will find each other soon. If I become a small child, I won't be able to get very far. Luckily I do not want to go very far. My work is here, and I'm too old to start over. When I go to their door with big dark eyes and a hungry look, I know they will take me in.

THE PRINCE

Guilt. Guilt. Guilt. My analyst keeps telling me I need to work out my feelings of guilt. Such nonsense. My mother died when I was born. I killed her. My father kept provoking wars so that he'd have to go away and fight them because he couldn't stand the sight of me, and no wonder, always reminding him.

And my dearest friend . . . So don't tell me not to feel guilty. I know all about guilt.

Most of the time I ignore it, of course. It helps to be a prince. The Prince, in fact. In the usual course of events, nobody gives me a bad time. They wouldn't dare. Even when I was a kid I did pretty much what I liked.

Correction. I did what Stephen liked. But that was what I liked too. Stephen was my tutor. Stephen taught me everything. I loved Stephen. I'll never *really* love anyone again.

I learned so much from Stephen. I was a lonely

kid, except for him. Oh, I saw lots of other young people. They were always being invited to the palace to keep me company. They were supposed to play with me, and they did. We did play, all very correct, all very distant—no fun ever. They could never forget I was the prince.

Such an ugly prince too. "Cross eyes, fat face, Nasty looks are your disgrace, You don't belong to the human race." That Ursula, that's what she used to whisper, to hiss; she sounded like a snake.

"You don't dare say that out loud," I'd tell her, and she would smile and close her mouth tight.

"I command you to beat Lady Ursula," I told Stephen one time. "She says insulting things to me."

"Nothing that I heard, my prince," Stephen responded gently. "But it's time Lady Ursula returned to her home." And when the abominable Ursula had been bundled off, Stephen smiled so tenderly. His eyes were luminous with unshed tears. "Come, my little prince," he murmured, "come now, let me prepare the perfumed footbath. Here, I'll add the oil. Let me instruct the musicians to play. Fear not, my little prince, they will not be offended by the sight of you. They will remain behind the arras at the far end of the hall. They will not see us or hear our talk. We will talk low, my prince, gentle music and gentle hands."

I would drift, totally relaxed, on the ocean of content, lulled by his hypnotic voice. "There, your feet in the footbath, so," he would continue, "and I rub in the perfumed oil, so, and I massage, gently, lov-

ingly, my princeling, so, and so, and so." Later it
would be Stephen's turn and I would perform the
same fond service for him as he had for me.

Oh, we were formal enough in public, always.
"What would I do without you, Stephen?" I sometimes asked.

"Ah, but you'll never be without me, my dear," he
always replied.

And I never was, from the time I was two years
old until I was nineteen. Is it only a year ago?

As I grew older, the servants gossiped about us. I
saw their sideways glances, heard the occasional
snicker. I was amused, but not for a moment troubled. No one could oust me; the king had no other
child. Perhaps I encouraged Ursula and her friends
to think that Stephen was my lover. Why not? It
wasn't true, but it would serve to keep Ursula and
her like at a distance. Tongues, even lying tongues,
weren't likely to wag loudly; my father was much
too quick to cut them off.

Sometimes I fantasized a life without Stephen,
just to experience the delicious thrill of fear. There's
nothing real to be afraid of, when you're a prince,
The Prince, even a fat, ugly prince, or so I thought.
But the pretense could make me shudder: What if
my father sent Stephen away?

Then I'd need to test my power. "More cream for
my coffee," I'd tell my valet. "Hop to it, or I'll send
you to the galleys."

I sent one of them to the galleys once, partly to
see if my orders would be obeyed, and partly so
they'd know I might carry out a threat and could do

it on a whim. I only had to whisper, after that, I only had to look, and they jumped to obey. It was fun for a month, and then it was a bore.

For entertainment, I ordered Lady Ursula to attend upon me. I put my arm around her and looked into her dull blue eyes. After a moment or two, I bent and kissed her. Her lips felt like jelly, like slime. What was she thinking? She tried to smile and flirt, but I could feel her trembling. Behind her eyelids I sensed the shudder of fear and the twin shudder of disgust. Part of me wanted to humiliate her into the ground. I saw myself ordering her to grovel on all fours, to bark like a dog.

I've never felt the least bit guilty about Ursula. But revulsion rose in me like vomit. I put weight into my words: "Faugh, you disgust me. Be banished from our court."

She went fast enough. So did they all. When my father got home from wherever the perennial battles were that year, only Stephen and I were left, Stephen and I and the servants and those few courtiers in service directly to the king who could not be dismissed.

He came early from the fighting that year. I was surprised. Stephen and I were surprised. My father found me on my knees by the footbath, head bent over my dear friend's precious feet. Stephen half-sat, half-lay on the padded couch.

What did my royal parent think he saw? His booted heel crunched the glass vial of perfumed oil. Viciously he kicked over the footbath. I stared up at him. I had nothing to blush for, but the treacherous blood boiled into my face all the same. Stephen started up, and his feet skittered on the oil-drenched floor. I grabbed at his knees, and he fell on top of me. My father eyed us, his face rigid with distaste. In the heavy silence he turned and stalked away.

Afterward I was certain the chamberlain must have sent word to him about Stephen and me, must have put lies in his head. So I wanted to experience fear, did I? Fool! All the power I thought I had was gone. The king refused to see me. Twice I wrote to him. My letters were returned, torn in little bits.

He confined me to my room, posting a guard. Once the door opened suddenly and my father stood framed in the entrance, somber in black velvet trimmed with pearls. "If I had another son to succeed me," he said bitterly, "I'd execute you too." I started forward, but he had already turned away. The door swung shut.

That was how I knew that Stephen was to die—or was already dead. They told me nothing. Then one day the guard took my tray and whispered in my left ear, "Tomorrow. The private court."

I bribed him with promises. "No, no, my prince," he said with a shudder when I offered him my ruby ring.

"You're right," I admitted. "Everyone knows it for mine." Bloodred, big as a pigeon's egg. I had nothing else to bargain with. For pity, for pity, he led me to the little upper window. I peered through ivy and saw the bag put over Stephen's head, saw the trap sprung and heard his neck bone snap. The feet, those dear, dear feet, vanished as the body dangled. It jerked for a minute or two, then swung with dreadful slowness. My own heart grew cold and colder as I watched.

"Come away then," whispered my guard at last, and half-led, half-carried me back to my room. Afterward I wondered if my father had planned that too, all of it, including my watching his hangman do his work.

The king left me alone for months after that, but there was no spring campaign next year. My father, for once, remained at home. I was allowed to exercise and to read, but had no company.

Then last May I was sent for. Urgently. Not to the audience room, but to His Majesty's private chamber.

I gazed at my father, propped in bed against a small mountain of pillows, his face as white as the lace that edged them. How extraordinary! In all the years of my life, it was the first time I had ever seen the man in bed.

Dreams of another life, a different life, chased each other through my head. Myself as a baby, suckled at my mother's breast. Myself as a little boy, jumping on my parents' bed—not that mahogany monstrosity with the vast posts and dark red velvet drapes, but an ordinary bed like the one in Stephen's room.

Angrily I pushed these visions away, like the fantasies, the lies they were. The rushes snapped under my boots as I strode forward. My father raised his hand as if to wave his attendants back, but the hand faltered. He raised his eyes, but the left eyelid drooped in dreadful parody of a wink.

"Closer," he whispered urgently, though I was already closer to him than I had been for many years, closer than I ever wished to be again.

His breath rasped as if he was in pain. Inwardly I smiled.

"I am not dead yet," he snarled. "Not yet, my son and heir. Heir! I have fought all my life to keep this kingdom and enlarge it. I will not die until the succession is secure. If you would rule soon, my son, you must find a mate, a female," he whispered, "and beget a child upon her. We will have a ball. They shall all be invited, and you, my son, shall choose. You shall choose or, I promise you, I will choose your wife myself."

I bowed. "Your wish is my command, my king." He read the mockery in my eyes.

I thought perhaps he would die of rage, but my father is too stubborn for that. Indeed, he has recovered much of his speech. His eyelid droops only slightly these days; the slackness is easy to miss.

A thousand invitations were sent. For days now pretty ladies have been arriving in their parents' company. The streets are clogged with coaches. Two dressmakers and at least one maiden have committed suicide, they tell me, because ball costumes were not finished in time.

Last night was the event. The same musicians played who made sweet music for Stephen and me. Then they were concealed by a heavy arras. The music sounded faintly. I never knew what a piercing noise it could make, even with thousands of guests in the vast ballroom.

I knew I'd hate dancing with the pretty ladies, even though Stephen had taught me well how the steps must go. Dutifully I whirled damsel after damsel over the polished floor. Could I stand to marry one? Perhaps, if she seemed empty enough, transparent enough. Perhaps.

Then suddenly I looked down. The current damsel was gloriously attired in something with pearls and ermine trim, but I hardly saw her dress. My eyes fixed on her feet.

Glass! I could see right through her shoes!

I stopped immediately. She almost fell. I steadied her. My eyes had not left her feet as they nestled like twin birds in their delicate little cages. Such feet! Oh, Stephen, you'd have loved them too. How I longed to put them into the footbath, to pour in the perfumed oil!

The music stopped. Everything stopped. It's hell being The Prince; no privacy at all. Everybody watching.

In the silence, the great clock began to chime. Alarmed, the damsel raised a hand to her cheek, then turned and ran. I ran after her through the mob of guests, across the peacock courtyard and down the wide marble stairs.

I kept my eyes on her feet. That is likely why I saw the glass slipper catch on the edge of the bottom step. It made a little chiming sound as it fell. I stooped for it, and in that second she was gone.

I sit here now with her slipper in my hand. When Stephen died, I was sure I'd never care for anyone again, but I must have—I will have—those feet. Guilt be damned! My father laughs, but he has permitted me to commandeer every town crier in the land. Tomorrow the great search begins. I must—I will—be satisfied.

Priscilla Galloway was born in Montreal and now lives in Metropolitan Toronto. She has taught literature and writing at the high-school and university levels and has been honored as Teacher of the Year by the Ontario Council of Teachers of English. Her published work includes a book of nonfiction for adults and a number of picture books for children. She has also edited several anthologies. Her own poetry and short fiction have appeared in small-press magazines and scholarly journals and have been broadcast by the Canadian Broadcasting Corporation.